TWO SISTERS

STORIES

Mehri Yalfani

TSAR
Toronto

We acknowledge the support of the Canada Council for the Arts for our publishing program. We also acknowledge support from the Ontario Arts Council.

"A Hand in the Cradle and a Foot in the Grave" was published previously in *In a Voice of Their Own: Stories by Iranian Women* (MAZDA, 1996); "Her Twin" in *Dandelion* (Volume 24, No. 2, 1997), "Happiness in Five Definitions" in *She's Gonna Be* (McGillan, 1998); and "Two Sisters" in French translation by Marguerite Anderson in *Virage* (No. 6, Summer 2000).

Cover art and design by Shirin Mohtashami

Canadian Cataloguing in Publication Data

Yalfani, Mehri
    Two sisters

ISBN 0-920661-84-X

I. Title.

PS8597.A47T96 2000   C 813'.54   C00-932181-0
PR9199.3.Y34T96 2000

Printed in Canada by Coach House Printing.

TSAR Publications
P. O. Box 6996, Station A
Toronto, Ontario M5W 1X7
Canada

ALSO BY THIS AUTHOR:

Parastoo (in English)
Happy Days (in Farsi)
Before the Fall (in Farsi)
Birthday Party (in Farsi)
Someone Is Coming (in Farsi)
The Shadows (in Farsi)
Far From Home (in Farsi)

ACKNOWLEDGEMENTS

Many thanks to Ann Decter, for her initial reading of the manuscript and suggestions. Also thanks to the Ontario Arts Council and the Canada Council for various grants.

Contents

In the Street of Solitude

When Mona saw the man on the balcony, she was surprised. Why, she thought, was the door open?

"Yes, it was," the man said, "you'd left it open for me. Have you forgotten about it?"

I can't lie, it's useless, Mona thought. It seems he knows about everything.

Every day Mona sat on the second-floor balcony, watching the street and saw the man crossing it. He seemed in his mid thirties, but she couldn't really guess how old he was. With his gray hair, long thin nose, tired look, skinny cheeks and his mouth hidden under his dark mustache. He walked with bent shoulders, ignoring the boys playing soccer in the street. Passing by her house, he stopped and watched the balcony.

Mona knitted. She was always busy with something in her hands, knitting or shelling peas or beans.

The man sat in front of her. He had a book in his hand.

"Would you like to look at it? It's an interesting book, the story of a lonely woman."

"Like me?"

"Like you."

Mona took a quick look at the book and returned it to the man.

"Don't you want to read it? It may amuse you and fill your loneliness."

My loneliness? Mona thought. She said nothing, watching the street. Everyday at this time, when the sunshine was playing with leaves of the orange tree. when the yard was full of shadow, when the noise of the children filled the street, and that twelve-year-old girl with long wavy ash-brown hair rode a bike in the street, the man passed by her house, walking alongside the wall. Reaching her house, he stopped and looked at her—sitting on the balcony and knitting. Her body was in shadow. Her hands were moving, knitting, shelling the peas.

Mona was absorbed by the street. She felt as if she had a fetus in her womb, moving, growing, getting born and going to the street, playing with other boys, making noises, riding a bike, his hair waving in the wind. Mona enjoyed her imagination, but a shadow of sadness covered her face.

"Your life seems empty without any children, " the man said.

Why does he call me you, Mona thought. Why is he so distant from me? What does he know about my real life?

"What do I know? Don't I come every night to your home? Every night when you go to bed with your husband, don't you place me in your bed? And then, you push your husband down from your bed and with me . . . "

Mona reddened. She made a move to leave the balcony. She should go to the kitchen to make the dinner. Her husband would come back home at ten, eleven o'clock or even later in the night. Taking his suit off, putting on his pajamas, Mona saw his hairy legs and turned her eyes away. He sat at the table, eating a plate full of food and belched loudly. Then he went to bed. Mona stayed in the kitchen, washed the dishes in silence. Sometimes she felt she wanted to scream. There were tears in her eyes as she made herself busy in the kitchen to be sure her husband fell asleep.

"If you had children from him," the man said, "it would be different."

"How?" Mona asked.

"In that case you would love him. He would be your children's father."

2

She lay down on the examination bed. The doctor's hands were cold, touching her body. Her muscles shrank. She wanted to shrink herself to prevent anybody from touching her.

"I can't examine you," the doctor said. "if you don't relax your muscles." She couldn't. The doctor's hand was a piece of icy iron. When it touched her skin, she shivered with hate and cold

The doctor was busy with the papers on his desk. He prescribed regular sex to increase her chance of becoming pregnant. The sweat of shame and disgust erupted from Mona's forehead. Her skirt's zipper stuck, she couldn't pull it up. Her eyes gazed at the doctor's hands, the swelling blue veins like routes on them.

"Perhaps it's his fault," the man said. "But he believes it's you that can't bear a child."

A barren land, he called her. A barren land, Mona thought.

Mona started to talk. She knew this man. Everyday he passed by her house.

"Talk," the man said. "It's necessary for you to talk. Talk about yourself. Don't be so closed. Talking may open a window to your closed life. You look like a locked case. Nobody knows what's going on inside you. You seem dumb with your silence. Words are made for human expression, but you don't want to use them. You just talk to yourself without using words, as I said, like a mute person. Talk, yes, talk."

"Talk?" Mona asked flushing. "For you? Who are you? I go sometimes to my sister's house and talk to her. My sister is a lucky woman. Her husband has left four children in her lap. She doesn't have even time to scratch her head. She always has something to do. Her husband is a witty man. When he's at home, he makes my sister laugh. He's a caring man, concerned about my sister and his children. He takes the children for walks. He helps my sister with chores. They are a happy family—really happy. I'm sure about it."

"And you envy her life?"

"I'm glad she's happy. But me . . . "

"You're not. If you had children, you might be a little happy, not

3

really happy, just a little."

"If I had children, I would be busy with them. I wouldn't have time to wonder what to do. I wouldn't need to sit in the balcony and stare at nothing, or look longingly at the children in the street."

"But you have a beautiful imagination. For example, when you sleep with me."

Mona reddened to her ears. An unusual anger was in her voice. "With you? When and where?"

"Don't feel shy," the man said. "No one knows about your affairs, even your husband. This is the space in which only you and I exist, and now . . . Do you like to sleep with me? I love you."

The man moved close to Mona. He took her face in his hands, stared at her eyes.

"You're a decent woman. Decent—like a domestic animal, like a horse, like a cow."

Tears were in Mona's eyes.

"It's not a beautiful analogy," the man said. "But you are. Don't be so decent."

"I can't be otherwise," Mona said. "Malevolence is not in my character."

"What about seduction?" the man asked.

"Seduction?"

Mona removed his hands. She wanted to say, What do you think of me? I'm not a bad woman. I'm not the kind of woman you have in your mind.

"Aren't you? What are you then? When you sleep with your husband without love or even with hate. When he forces you to . . . "

Mona reddened again. Sweat covered her forehead. The doctor's cold hands made her body shiver as if cold metal had touched her.

"Relax your muscles," the doctor said.

The doctor's office was gloomy and the nurse had a steely smile on her face, without compassion.

She looked at the street. Boys started to fight, scream and hit each other. The girl with her ash-brown hair stood in a corner and watched them. A woman put out her head from a window and shouted, "Bahram, Bahram." And then she shut the window.

In a moment she'll go to the street to scream at the children, Mona thought.

It was always the same, the children's play ended with fighting and hitting. That was the street rule—always the same rule. Her solitude was filled by the street, eventually fighting occurred. The girl with the bike wasn't there any longer. Her mother had called her back home.

Night invaded the street. More people went back home. Darkness covered the balcony and absorbed Mona. A cold breeze passed over her skin. She collected her knitting, went into the room, waited for her husband to come home.

"You have a boring life," the man said. "Why don't you read? Why don't you write?"

"Write? What about?"

"About yourself. You've a wonderful imagination. Every night when you make love with me, I really enjoy it. Why don't you try these adventures? For example, spending one night in a desert by yourself, meet a man whom you don't know, spend the whole night with him, watching the stars, reciting poetry and narrating tales."

"How do you know these things?"

"How do I know? Am I not always with you?"

"Not always, not everywhere. You're my man, but you're not perfect. You're like other men, you have some weaknesses."

"But you accepted me."

"I don't have another choice."

"Look. It's not always the men who aren't perfect. You're imperfect as well. You imagined me for yourself. I'm your man, but still I've weaknesses. Why don't you imagine a perfect man?"

"I can't."

"Why?"

"I don't know. Men are complicated, too demanding. Sometimes I think I'd better give up. Live by myself. But you know."

Mona became quiet. Her hands were still busy knitting—though Mona didn't look at what she was knitting. She realized she was doing wrong—but she didn't care. She just wanted to be busy with something. When her hands were busy, her imagination was stimulated, making fantastic dreams that she enjoyed.

The man leaned over the fence. He stood in such a manner that Mona could see his profile. The balcony wasn't in absolute darkness. The street lights were on and the first-floor balcony light, which Mona had turned on the night before and forgot to turn off in the morning.

Mona looked at the man. He no longer seemed a real person. He was like a shadow leaning over the fence.

Why should I have to dream up a man? Mona thought, what's the wrong with my real life? My only problem is that I don't have children. So that's not a big deal. My sister who has four children, what happiness has she? She has to labour day and night like a horse. Her husband is very bossy, he always nags at her. Why did I tell him that my brother-in-law was a witty man? He's always in a bad mood, always in debt. My poor sister with four children has to get along with so much misery, always worries about her children's future. I, who have no worries, why am I not happy?

The man returned and looked at her, "It's your husband's fault. You don't love him."

Mona wanted to say, When he sleeps with me, he calls me a barren land. He says no water will flourish in a barren land. But she stayed quiet.

"You suffer from his contemptuous behaviour," the man said. "Why don't you leave him? You have your man."

"My man?" Mona laughed loudly. "My man! I told you, you're not perfect. So then, what do I expect from my husband?"

"So you are pleased with your situation. Every evening sitting on this balcony, watching the neighbourhood, the street, and envying other women."

"You're wrong," Mona said. "I don't envy anybody. I don't have anything to do with others."

"As I said, you're a decent domestic animal, busy with yourself. Decent like a horse."

"I was telling you, I watch the street every evening. Boys playing soccer."

A pale joy shimmered on her face.

"Why are you smiling?" the man asked.

"Do you see my face in this darkness?"

Mona wasn't knitting any more. Her knitting was abandoned on her lap, but her hands were playing with the thread, making knots and untying them.

"Yes, I see," the man said, "I see that you're happy. I know you imagine one of those boys for yourself. That one who has soft brown hair, pale skin and a tiny body. You don't know his mother and don't want to know her. You don't know which house he lives in. Perhaps he comes from another neighborhood."

The man became quiet. Mona too was quiet. She really imagined one of those boys was hers. Every night as she waited for her husband to come home, she had the boy to herself. She fed him his dinner, sent him to bed, read him tales, poetry, talked to him, asked him about school and friends. All the time a smile on her face. When she heard her husband's car braking in the parking lot, her smile disappeared. She became sulky and ignorant as usual.

"Why don't you choose a girl?" the man asked.

"I don't want to," Mona answered without hesitation.

"Do you hate your gender?"

"No, I don't hate it. I'm worried about a girl's future. I'm afraid she'll be miserable like me."

"You see, " the man said, "you confess that you live in misery. Why don't you change that?"

Mona was quiet. The man as well. There was a heavy atmosphere between them. The man looked at Mona. Mona collected her knitting. The man left the balcony and went into the room.

Where is he going? Mona thought, does he want to stay here tonight? What do I tell my husband?

The man was at the door by now. He turned.

"Don't worry. I won't stay here. If I do, what are you afraid of? He can't see me."

"Please go," Mona said.

"No need to ask. You see that I'm leaving."

Mona heard his steps going down the stairs. Then she saw him in the semidark yard with his shoulders bent and a book under his arm. He opened the half-closed gate of the yard, stayed for a while in the doorway and looked at her. Mona saw a smile on his face.

"Shall I follow him?" she thought.

She dismissed the thought. The man disappeared, leaving the gate open behind him. Mona climbed down the stairs hurriedly.

The Morning of the Fifth Day

Nasrin is restless. She has decided to send her fourteen-year-old son out of the country. In fact, he's not fourteen yet, just thirteen years and eight months.

Last night she couldn't get to sleep. "He's our guest for five more days only," she says.

"Not five days, four, " I say, "the morning of the fifth day, he'll be gone."

She sighs. "That's right. The morning of the fifth day, he'll be gone."

She's frizzling like incense on fire, spinning around herself. She's vice-principal at a school and has taken this week off. The principal treats her well. She goes shopping several times a day, buying many things, spending money like pebbles.

"What's the use of this junk?" I tell her, "wool socks, shampoo, soap, and toothpaste!"

"He needs them," she answers me angrily, "everything is expensive over there."

Ever since she heard that sending fourteen-year-old boys out of the country is forbidden, it's as if she's on fire. She wants to send him away as soon as possible, afraid he'll be taken to the war front.

"It will be a long time before he can become a soldier," I say, "he's just thirteen."

"Time will pass in a twinkle," she says, "when the war began, he was nine. Now he's thirteen. When he's eighteen, he has to go to the war. There's no escape. Perhaps they'll take him from school. Haven't you seen the many thirteen- and fourteen-year-old boys on television? They look like girls. They still have high voices. It's war. It's not a joke."

She's right. It's not easy to send a young boy to the frontline. A boy like Omid, he's such a spoiled boy. Nasrin raised him like that, because he came after the three girls. He looks naive. I did the same. Now, we have to send him away.

"What can we do," Nasrin asks, "leave him here until they come and take him away? Or until they stop him from leaving? And then to the front line?"

She's right. When he finishes high school, he will have no choice, except to go to the war. Elaheh always said that he should get accepted into the university, to have an excuse not to go to the war.

Nasrin sneered. She didn't say anything in front of Omid. But when Elaheh was arrested, she remarked, "University? Ha! She was accepted. Her marks were more than ninety percent."

Elaheh failed the investigation. Then she was arrested. We didn't know why.

"They arrested her without any reason," Nasrin says, "she's done nothing, except read too much and study hard."

Elaheh hasn't been to trial yet and we don't know why she's in jail.

"I always feel anxious," Nasrin says, "as if vinegar is boiling in me. I'm afraid they won't let him go."

"Why not?" I comfort her. "There's no reason to prevent him. He has his passport, his visa, and we've paid the exit fee for him. Just four days left before he is gone."

"Yes, the morning of the fifth day, he'll be gone, " she says. "I wish that day would come sooner. I wish these four days would vaporize into the sky." She ponders and says, "If they hadn't arrested Elaheh, I would send her too."

"With what money?" I ask. "We cannot afford to send him away."

She ponders. She's absentminded. She looks destitute. She cries, but not in front of Omid.

"We have become miserable," she says, "when he's gone, it'll be the beginning of our problems. It's not easy. I was there, in Germany, they don't treat foreigners well. They don't consider refugees human beings like themselves."

Nasrin's talk pains me too. I want to say, "Isn't it better to give up and let him be in the hands of God. Let what is going to be, be."

But I say nothing. I know she's against it. She wants to send him out of the country. She has it in her mind to save the child. She has a right to be afraid, she's afraid they'll send him to the frontline, or arrest him.

"Nobody has anything to do with a thirteen-year-old child," I say.

She shakes her head and looks at me strangely. Like a wise person gazing at a fool. Perhaps she wants to say, There's no difference between thirteen and eighteen for them. Elaheh was just eighteen. She finished high school and passed the university exams, but failed in the investigation. And then they arrested her. Why?

Nasrin asks, "Why did they arrest her? She had done nothing. She was a smart girl. She wasn't guilty, was she? They just found some books with her. I wish I could have sent Elaheh too, she's smart, and she's clever. I hope she can take out her Klim from the water[1] over there too."

Nasrin becomes quiet, dreamy.

"Don't be too anxious," I say, "you'll kill yourself."

"No, don't worry," she says, "we women are strong. We have a thick skin. We know how to stand up to any situation. Haven't Elham and Afsaneh gone far away? Do you see them having any problems?"

"Far away?" I say. "They haven't left Iran. There's the telephone in your hand. You can talk to them whenever you want. They can come to see you. Omid has to go far away. So far that he can't come back. He has to go away and be a refugee. A refugee is someone who can't return to his own homeland."

She shakes her head and says, "Homeland? What's the use of homeland where you're not safe, where your children are in danger

11

for nothing, where they're threatened with being sent to the frontline, or to jail for having some books. What's the use of this war? I don't want my child being killed for nothing or for a key to paradise.[2] Which paradise? I don't believe in their paradise. They made life a hell for us and want to send our children to paradise. I prefer to send my child to a foreign country to be a refugee and never come back, rather than be killed for nothing. I have hope for him. He may become someone over there. Maybe . . . "

Then she becomes quiet. There are lots of things she is thinking about, restlessly, as if she's sitting on a fire.

"I wish Omid were a girl too," she says, "if he was a girl, I would have just one sorrow—that I don't have a son. But now it's hard."

I look at her with sympathy.

"Women are stronger," she says." Do you remember when I married you. I moved to your city, Maragheh.[3] I couldn't speak Turkish. It seemed that I had traveled into a foreign country. I didn't understand one word of your language. But I learned it very quickly. The language soaked into me like oil into paper."

"Learning the language isn't a big problem," I say. "He'll learn it too."

"It's not the language," she says."Assimilating into a new society is hard for men. We women had to learn how to do it. We learned it generation after generation. We were always the ones who had to leave our father's homes. You have always been under your parents' protection, in your own home. But we women had to leave, we had to assimilate into a new home."

Nasrin worries. Anxiety doesn't leave her alone. She doesn't talk about Elaheh. I'm sure she thinks about her. She thinks about Afsaneh and Elham, too. In the last few days she has called them several times. They're supposed to come. Afsaneh's daughter is sick. She may not come. But Elham is coming. She wanted to come by the night bus.

"Don't come by the night bus," Nasrin screamed at her, "your child will get sick!"

Elham has a boy, six months old. Afsaneh has two daughters. She would like to have a son too.

"What do you want to do with a boy?" Nasrin says, "When he grows up, he'll have thousands of problems. He'll have to go to military service or leave the country."

She says nothing about Elaheh. She talks about everything except Elaheh, because she doesn't want to disturb Omid's feelings. When Omid asks about Elaheh, Nasrin says, "When she is released, I'll tell her to write to you."

"Send her out, too," Omid says, "promise me you'll send her too."

"I'll see," Nasrin says.

"Elaheh is intelligent," Omid says. "If she goes there, she'll certainly be accepted in the university."

He dreams. I can't understand what kind of imagination he has about the outside. He'll be a refugee there. Ahmad has done the works. It's eight or nine years since Ahmad has been living there. He has a German wife. He knows what to do.

*

The morning of the fifth day arrives.

Nasrin was talking about Elaheh yesterday. She was waiting for her call. There was no call. Since they arrested her, she has called once and said that she's alright and she may be released after two-three months. She said these things to her mother. I wasn't at home that day. I was at work, driving my car as a taxi. My salary is not enough any more. Sometimes I think maybe Nasrin just imagined it and Elaheh hasn't called at all.

Nasrin waited all day yesterday for Elaheh's phone call. Elham and Afsaneh believed her, too. Elham said, "Does she call frequently?"

Nasrin didn't answer her. She was absentminded. All day there were comings and goings at home. The telephone rang too. Nasrin answered the phone. She was waiting. I don't know why she was so optimistic.

*

Omid left two hours ago. We came back home. Nasrin is quiet. Very quiet. She was close to crying at the airport. But she didn't. She controlled herself. She cried on the way back home, but not very much. Afsaneh and Elham didn't let her cry. Her mother was there, too. Everyone is here. More people are coming. We had been home a half hour, when the telephone rang. Nasrin's eyes widened. "Is it Omid? Didn't they let him get on the airplane?"

I took the receiver. It wasn't Omid. Omid had gone. We stayed at the airport until we heard the announcement that the airplane had taken off. Perhaps now it's out of Iran's skies. He will be a refugee tomorrow or the day after tomorrow. We don't know when we can see him again. Ahmad wrote that it will take a year or two until his case is cleared, but his life isn't in danger.

It was a strange man on the line.

"Are you Elaheh Imani's father?"

"Yes, I am," I said.

My heart was in my mouth. Elaheh probably wanted to talk to me. I was lucky I was at home. The man's voice interrupted my thought.

He was talking. What was he saying? Talking about Elaheh's body and her will. I passed the phone to Afsaneh. I mean Afsaneh took the phone from me. I didn't understand what was happening. Everywhere was dark. I was giddy. Then I heard someone screaming.

Was it Afsaneh, Elham, or Nasrin? I didn't know. I leaned against the wall.

The phone rings. The doorbell rings. How noisy it is here. The morning of the fifth day arrived, too. I said to Nasrin, "Don't worry, it will finally arrive."

NOTES

1. A certain kind of carpet, not very expensive.

2. A key that was given to the soldiers going to the frontline; if they were killed they could go to paradise with it.

3. One of the cities of Iran where the population speaks Turkish.

Arman

A storm arrived
and stole my footprint.

SOHRAB SEPEHRI

Minoo came out of the kitchen and looked out the window. She saw a
winter sky with a black cloud which deepened the dark. She strolled
over to the window and pulled the curtains. Vahid, her husband,
leaned back on the sofa, his head on the back cushion, watching TV.
Minoo stopped near the dining table. A few minutes ago, when she
collected the supper dishes, the TV was off. Vahid had been in
Arman's room. Minoo had washed the dishes thinking about what
had happened since the afternoon. She was concerned about Arman,[1]
how Vahid would talk to him and make him understand.

She stared at the darkness behind the window for a while. Her
apartment was on the twenty-first floor in a high-rise at the edge of
the city. Her view was a barren land and a grove, both dark in the
night. A highway stretched in the distance, cars like ghosts passing in
the darkness with two lit eyes before they were lost in the night.

Minoo turned to watch the TV. Two men, one with dark, thick eyebrows and a strong face, and the other with a sweat-red face and a
stout body, were brutally assaulting a third man with fists and kicks.
The third man was like a boxing bag, thrown this way and that. He

was knocked to the ground with a heavy fist. The black man hit his face. The camera showed a close-up, the face was deformed. The man groaned like an animal. Minoo turned from the TV to Vahid, who was absorbed by the film. An unwanted anger grasped her. The man's face falling on the ground was disgusting, but the two other men looked at him indifferently. Words stuck to Minoo's tongue. A cigarette between Vahid's fingers, with its ashes on the verge of dropping. She wanted to say, "Be careful." She wanted to say, "Turn the TV off." She didn't. She just gazed at the TV, now showing a street. Then the two men getting in a car, driving away.

The cigarette ashes dropped on Vahid's black sock and spread like spit.

"Turn it off." Minoo said. But she didn't know if she meant the cigarette or the TV, or if Vahid didn't hear her or heard her and didn't care. Minoo looked out the window, at the darkness and lights glimmering far away. Vahid drew on his cigarette and kept in the smoke and watched the TV, its sound low. The only sound in the room.

The camera zoomed in again on the fallen man. His face was out of shape and motionless. A stream of blood passed from his swollen lips. The street was dark.

"Turn it off," Minoo said loudly.

Vahid regained himself and looked at Minoo, but he didn't acknowledge her. Minoo was angry, she didn't know whether at the violent film or at Vahid's insensitivity, his sitting on the sofa, relaxing as if nothing had happened. She turned the TV off and stood beside it. She stared at Vahid with his back to the darkness outside. From where she stood, she couldn't see car lights in the darkness, there was just the overcast sky of the cold weather. The wind howled like a savage wolf. A sudden fear rushed her—fear of the illusive, dark atmosphere outside the window.

Indifferent to her, Vahid turned the TV on again with the remote control. Two uniformed men put the fallen man who might be dead or alive on a stretcher, pushed him in an ambulance and, in another shot, carried him into a hospital. Police were there, too. There was vacancy on all the faces, the same vacancy as on Vahid's face.

"Turn it off!" she screamed.

Vahid looked at her, surprised. He ignored her. With a sharp movement Minoo turned the TV off, took the remote control from Vahid's hand and tossed it towards the window and the darkness. It hit the rocking chair before hitting the window and falling. Minoo shivered. The window could have broken, and cold and wind would have rushed into the room. She looked at Vahid, sat down on the sofa, and sobbed.

Vahid looked at her, wondering. He moved close to her, hugged her and said, "What's the matter? Why are you crying?"

Minoo wiped the tears from her face with her palm. She wondered why she had lost control, so unpredictably. She tried not to, but she thought again about what had happened. She still couldn't believe it. She remembered Arman's face, his looking at her, when she gave him the explanation. He didn't want to see his father. He hid himself in his room, put the chair behind his door and sat on it to prevent his father going in. He wouldn't look his father in the eyes, didn't want to listen to him. She didn't know if he believed what his father had told him or not. He wasn't a child any more. He was eleven years old. They had told him many times that he was a big man, to give him confidence to understand more for his age.

The room was full of silence. Minoo was exhausted and needed Vahid to talk to her. A vague question sat with her that she couldn't utter.

She looked at Vahid, who seemed indifferent. He lit another cigarette, puffed at it and sent the smoke out like a delicate cloud. Instead of the question which had occupied her mind, she asked, "Why did you lie to the child?"

Vahid didn't answer. He was busy with his own thoughts. The question opened a way for conversation. Minoo asked louder, "I'm talking to you. Why did you lie to him?"

Vahid leaned away from her. For a while he stared at Minoo's eyes. Minoo noticed shame in his look, shame she hadn't seen before. In

Vahid's eyes there had always been pride, intentional or not. Ever since the first time she met him in the hospital—in a resident's uniform, with disheveled hair as if he had just taken the surgery hat off his head, and his sleeves rolled up—as he came out of the operation room. She was a nurse in the surgery department then. When they met each other in the hall way there was pride in his eyes. Pride and joy. They got to know each other more. She had seen that pride and joy often in his eyes. And now instead of pride there was shame that made her ashamed too. She wasn't innocent either. But she wanted Vahid to explain it to her. It was like a problem which should be solved. A problem which had been with her for more than eight months, it was with them both, and they knew that one day they should solve it. But they postponed that out of fear. They hoped the problem would be solved by itself. Now not only had the problem not been solved, but also it had became more complicated.

Vahid stayed where he was, leaning back. Even his hands looked helpless—extinguishing the cigarette in an ashtray and then abandoned on his knees.

"Do you think it was my fault?" he asked.

"Whose was it then?" Minoo asked, "Was it I who deceived the child with big lies?"

"No, it wasn't you. It was me. But, well, I didn't mean it."

"But you misled the child."

"Yes, I did. But you aren't without fault either. You could have told him the truth. So you're guilty as well."

Minoo sat a little further and became quiet. Yes, she was guilty as well. She could have told the truth, why didn't she?

"Yes, you're guilty, too," Vahid said, "you too never told Arman what work you do at the hospital."

"What are you talking about?" Minoo asked. "My fault is not as big as yours. You lied to him. You told him you're a surgeon. I didn't tell him anything."

"Did you tell him what you do at the hospital?"

"He never asked me that I had to tell him anything."

"And if he had asked, would you have told him?"

Minoo didn't answer. She asked herself, "Would I have? Would I have told him the truth?"

Minoo had told her friends and acquaintances that she was working in the hospital, but she didn't say what she was doing. She had told Vahid, anger in her voice, "We came here to have a better life. We thought we could progress here and find a place. And now with this job! I'm an educated nurse. Why don't they accept me? Why should I do the job of an uneducated person?"

Vahid soothed her, "Wait for a while. It'll be all right. Let me pass my exams, get my license and work as a real surgeon, then . . . But we didn't come here to become anything. When we fled home, we just wanted to save our lives. We didn't think about these other things."

"But well—"

"That's it. We should get along with it, and we have to try and do our best to get our proper status."

Minoo was thoughtful.

"Tell me," Vahid asked her, "Don't be shy. Why didn't you tell him the truth?"

"I couldn't. How could I tell him what I'm doing in the hospital. He thinks I'm a nurse. Well, I am. Am I not?"

"Yes, you are. Damned be the one who denies it. I'm a surgeon, too, am I not?"

"But here you're not a surgeon. I mean you tried to be, but you couldn't."

"What am I then? A butcher?"

Minoo looked at him and said nothing. But her eyes said, Yes you are a butcher, aren't you?

Vahid continued, "Yes, I'm a butcher. I have to be a butcher, to win our bread."

Minoo put her hand on his knee and looked at him with sympathy.

"I didn't say you're a butcher."

"So what? Why are you so upset?"

"You know very well why I'm upset. What do we do with Arman?"

19

Vahid said impatiently, "I don't know what I'm going to do with him. You just accept that I had to—"

"You had to lie to the child?"

"No, I had to be a butcher. I had no choice. You saw how much I tried. For five years, it was an ordeal. For five years I just dreamed about it and tortured myself about passing the exams. You saw that I had to accept any job for survival and I studied and I did any dirty volunteer job in the hospital with the hope that I could be a surgeon here, but it didn't work. So what could I do then? Hang myself? I had to live. So you'd better know that I like butchery. It's like surgery. Not much difference between them. The only difference is, with a human being, when you split his body, you want to put it together again. You should cure it, take a lump out of it and sew it again, or take a sick organ and replace it with a healthy one. But with the butchery it's a little different. When you have a carcass in your hands, you must cut it into pieces; take out its organs and sell them to people and make good money. You see that since I became a butcher we have a better life."

He had a bitter smile on his face and continued, "Yes, not too much difference. When I hold the butchery knife in my hand and dissect a lamb or a cow carcass, I remember the time I was in Pars hospital and opened a person's stomach."

Minoo stared at Vahid. It seemed to her that she didn't know the man. A sneer on his face; his mustache umkempt, his thick black eyebrows, his big body, all the features of a butcher. She had gone several times to his butcher shop and seen him with a stained apron and plastic gloves, standing behind the counter with a big knife in his hand and chatting with the customers in a superior mood, bluffing about the meat he offered them. She sometimes tried to remember him in Pars hospital, behind the operating table, only his eyes visible behind the surgery mask and a smile in them. Or when she went to see him with Arman at five. Vahid in his white uniform authoritatively talking to a nurse.

Over eight months the man had changed slowly from a surgeon

into a butcher. When he came home, the smell of fat and blood suffused his whole body. He went directly to the bathroom, to wash himself and change his clothes. If he had a good day and good business, he told some jokes he had heard from his customers and made Arman and her laugh. He told Arman about the surgeries he did, the feet he cut, hearts and livers he had taken out, and Arman believed that he was working in the hospital as a surgeon.

Arman asked his mother where she worked and she said at the hospital, the child was happy with his parents' jobs. But Minoo never had the courage to tell him what she did at the hospital.

Minoo stared at Vahid. She released herself from disturbing thoughts and said, "What should we do now? Now that he knows the truth, do you think he's lost his faith in us? This afternoon, when he came home, you weren't home to see how he cried, saying I won't believe you any more."

Vahid was quiet. Minoo said, "Ha? What do we do with him?"

"I don't know."

"How did he find out about it? Why did he come to your store? He didn't know where your store was. He didn't know you have a store."

"I don't know. That goddamn Kiumars brought him. Perhaps his father told him about my store. He has seen my ad in the newspaper. You know, his father is a surgeon, too. He too hasn't been able to pass the exams. He might have wanted revenge."

"Revenge? What revenge? Have you done something to him?"

"Last week he came to my store. I told him, man, you'd be better off to have a store in some other part of this city, not to forget you've been a surgeon. Instead of delivering pizza or driving a taxi, have a butcher shop. I told him a butcher has a connection with surgery that other jobs don't. I think he was offended and spoke to his son. His son is in the same school as Arman. Arman said he called him a liar in front of all the students and told them that his father wasn't a surgeon."

"Well, what if he doesn't want to go to school tomorrow?"

Vahid didn't answer.

"Ha? Have you thought about that? If he says, I'm not going to school, what are we going to do?"

"Why wouldn't he go to school?"

"You said that Kiumars called him a liar and mocked him. What if other students mock him too? He was saying this evening, I'm not going to school any more. Have you thought about that?"

"Yes I did," Vahid said after a while.

"What?"

"I'll change his school. We'll move from this neighborhood. We'll move to an area where no Iranis live, a place far from here. A place where no one knows us."

"And will you tell him again that you're a surgeon?"

"No, it's no use to lie to him. He knows about my job. Why should I lie to him? Now, it's your turn to think about telling him the truth."

"What do you mean?"

"I mean you should tell him what you do at the hospital."

"If he asks—"

"If he asks, you should tell him that you're not a professional nurse."

"Am I not?"

"No, you are not. You were, when I was a surgeon. But now, none of us are what we once were. We should accept what we are and our child should accept it too."

"Well, is the point the kind of job we do? The point is that we—"

"Yes, the point is that we saved our lives, and now we are alive and we—"

Minoo didn't hear the rest of Vahid's words. She was thinking, if they hadn't come here . . .

And then she yearned for the past. The days when Vahid and she met. She was a nurse, Vahid a resident in the surgery department. She said, "I was thinking, if we hadn't come here, now you and I would be some people important. Perhaps I would be head nurse of a department and you—a well-known surgeon."

Vahid looked at her in silence. It wasn't clear whether he was listening. Minoo, enthralled by her own thoughts, continued, "And we wouldn't have had to lie to our Arman."

She waited for Vahid to say something. She asked, "What are you thinking about?"

"I was thinking, one forgets everything so quickly. You've forgotten that we had to flee. Forgotten that we had to abandon everything and escape in the night. And if we hadn't, now we would either be in jail or under ground or worse, repentants who didn't know ourselves.

Minoo said with a sadness in her words, "And perhaps we couldn't have had the chance to have our Arman."

Then she rushed to the bathroom to wash away her tears.

NOTE

1. Arman is a male name and means a spiritual goal.

Parvin

They were sitting in a bar downtown. His father had arrived three days ago. The first day he looked tired and baffled. The long trip from home had left its marks on his face. But now he seemed refreshed. He even seemed younger. When he looked at his father in the pale orange light of the bar, he could see the traces of ten years of aging in the crevices of his mouth, his eyes. He ordered beer for himself, whiskey on ice for his father, his favorite drink. Before the revolution they always had a few bottles in the house. After dinner he would sip a glass of whiskey while leafing through the newspaper.

The bar seemed empty. Further away, a man and a woman were sitting at a table, the woman had her long blonde hair in a pony tail. She had a mini skirt on and her long well-shaped thighs were on display. His father would look at those thighs every now and then and smile. He could plainly see the lecherous look in his face. His smile upset him. He moved his chair to block his father's view.

In the three days that he had been here, his father had spoken about Iran in fragments. He had told him the general news and the family news. He talked about Mojgan and her twin daughters: Taraneh and Somaieh, who were growing up and who missed their uncle. He showed him their snapshots taken with Mojgan and her husband. He showed him a picture of his mother, wearing a veil, standing by the sea. Another picture of Mehran and his wife and their two sons, each of whom had turned into a young man.

All this time, Siavash hadn't asked about Mahtab and his father hadn't said anything. Mahtab was like a forgotten tale, a fable. A fable that he had once heard and forgotten all about later. Now with his father present he could remember the whole story once again. He wanted to remember every little detail, but he wanted to forget too, to let go. He didn't know if his father thought of her too. Maybe he didn't want to be reminded of Mahtab, a grandchild who was in his life for only a day, maybe he didn't want to believe in her existence.

A third glass of beer and a second whiskey on ice for his father, who looked flushed with a smile on his face. He moved in his seat every few minutes to have a good look at the blonde woman. Siavash turned to look at the woman too. Smoking a cigarette, she was chatting with the man at her table.

"This is a good country, you should be thankful that you are here," his father said still smiling.

"How do you mean?"

"Everything," he replied, blinking. "I am so happy that you are successful now, and your life is settled here. Back home it is very harsh, specially for young people."

His father's approval meant nothing to him.

"What about Mahtab?" he asked. "Do you have any news of her? Do you ever see her?"

"Mahtab? Which Mahtab?"

He blushed. "Mahtab? Don't you know her? Your own grandchild?" his voice started shaking.

His father didn't answer, his eyes locked into his son's. They stared at each other for a few seconds.

"So you don't know anything about her?"

"How about yourself? Do you have any news?"

"Me?"

He didn't have any news either. Mahtab's grandmother would send him a picture of her along with a short letter every time he sent them some money. He would bury the pictures among the pages of a book. Then when she had started school she wrote too, with her crooked handwriting. "My dearest father"—that was how she started her letters. Each new year he would receive a greeting card signed by herself: Mahtab.

The last greeting card had a haft siin table. He had shown it to Susan and told her all about the new year ceremony. Susan had listened but he could see that she didn't understand much of what he had said. She had asked who Mahtab was. At first he didn't want to answer, but then said flatly: "My daughter."

*

It was more than four months since his father had come, a fine morning in the fall and the sun was shining through the windows, lighting parts of the living room. His father was clean shaven and smelled of after-shave. He was sitting on the couch. Susan stepped out of the shower, she had her short-sleeved, V-necked T-shirt and jeans on. Her tanned young skin was radiant, her straight shining hair smelled of chamomile. She sat beside the father and put her feet up on the table. The father talked to her in his broken English. Susan laughed, her small white teeth sparkling. Her narrow eyes became even narrower when she laughed. She would put her small white hand on the father's thighs and would repeat with a thick accent the Persian words she had learned from him.

Siavash was preparing breakfast. The father looked at his son who was in his own world, ignoring them. He had set the table, and when the eggs and toast were done, he put them on the table and called them. The father would say something in English or Persian and Susan would laugh and move her head. Siavash drank his coffee in silence.

"Why aren't you having any breakfast?" his father asked

"I dreamt of Parvin last night." He answered.

"Parvin?" his father replied. "The star Parvin you mean?"

Siavash felt bitter and looked at his father.

"No, not the star. My wife, Parvin."

"Oh," his father said and swallowed hard. He drank some coffee and looked at Susan, who couldn't understand a word of what they had just said. Her small eyes seemed to be sinking in her eye sockets and her lips were thin. Her skin had no blemishes, like a white piece of paper, she looked like those plastic dolls that you could buy in the bazaar for a few coins.

"I dreamt that she came to Canada, we were living together. Mahtab was here too, she was growing up, she looked so much like Parvin."

His father brought the coffee mug to his lips; he didn't drink though, he put it back on the table.

"So you don't visit my daughter? You are ignoring her?"

His father didn't reply.

"You don't want to accept her either?"

His father looked at him and for a few seconds their eyes met.

"You never wanted to accept her, she was my wife and you didn't want her," Siavash said, "not you, or mother. I don't blame my mother, she always looked up to you, but you?"

There was silence between them for a while. Susan took her mug and sat on the couch, she turned on the TV and the sound of cartoons filled the room. Siavash looked at Susan and said, "Turn that down." His voice was harsh and commanding. Susan turned off the TV set. Taking her coffee with her, she went to the bedroom. When she passed Siavash, hesaid: "I am sorry."

Susan touched his shoulder: "It's OK."

"Why did you have to hurt her?" his father said. "She is a nice girl."

"It doesn't matter now."

A few minutes passed in silence. Siavash was turning the coffee mug in his hand.

"Why do you dwell on the past?" his father asked. "What ever there was, it is all finished now. You have a good life now, you found a nice girl, why don't you marry her? Your mother will be happy. The old woman is worried about you."

Siavash thought, "The old woman?" He remembered his mother. How old was she now? He wanted to ask, but he didn't. She didn't look like an old woman to him, even in her picture by the sea.

"How about you?" he asked, "You were worried about me?"

"I was, but that was before I came to see you, not now. God bless you, everything seems fine. You have finished your studies, you are an engineer, you have a good job, you found a nice girl . I heard Chinese women are very good housekeepers, they take good care of their husbands."

"So you think I have no worries anymore?"

His father put a piece of pita bread in his mouth and stared at him. The fun had fled from his face. "What worries you my son? You are happy now? Do you know if you were back home how you would have ended up? I wish you could see Mehran, how hard he works, and Mojgan, poor Mojgan! She has to go to work with Maghaneh, covering herself from head to toes. She is an engineer too, for God's sake, but they were going to fire her just because they thought she wasn't wearing her veil properly. She says her boss is a young fellow who has just graduated from college and doesn't even know his left hand from his right, and he is constantly bugging her. You don't know what is going on there. You are lucky that you are here."

"So you don't go and visit Mahtab? Do you ever see her?"

"Why are you thinking about Mahtab today? I've been four months here, you have never mentioned her before, did you get off the wrong side of bed today?"

"I dreamt of her last night. You and mother looked at her in disdain. Why? Why didn't you accept her? Was it because she was two years older than me? Or because she didn't have a father. She was renting and didn't have her own home, or was it because she was not so pretty?"

"It wasn't that. You were so young then, you were almost a kid."

"I was nineteen, I was hardly a kid."

"You hadn't finished your studies yet, hadn't gone to university, hadn't gone to the army, don't you remember?"

"Those aren't the reasons for you to throw her out, not accept her as my wife."

"Yes she was your wife, but your mother and I were against your marriage to Parvin. You weren't a man yet."

"But I loved her."

"Young love . . . "

"I married her. She got pregnant, but you didn't want to see her. You weren't kind to her, so I had to cut my relationship with you. You still ignored us, you eliminated me from your lives, that was why I didn't go to university like Mehran and Mojgan did. I didn't become an engineer. I didn't get a good job. I had to work in construction. I had to become a porter, yes I didn't tell you, but I worked in Bazaar as a porter, but I wasn't ashamed of all that. I loved my wife—she was working too. She worked in a factory. We lived in one room downtown, Shoosh Square. Those nine, ten months you didn't even once come to visit us. You didn't ask about us, you didn't want to know if we were dead or alive. If we were hungry or not, you didn't want to care and you didn't care. Your house had empty rooms, the third floor was all empty. Parvin mentioned it a few times to me, but I said no. I preferred to stay where I was, in that one rented room and not ask anything from my own parents, and she accepted that.

"Yes I was not an engineer like Mehran and Mojgan, and my wife was not a pretty wife like Mehran's wife, she didn't have rich parents, she didn't even have a father, she hadn't graduated from high school, and her parents' house like Mojgan's in-laws was not in a rich neighborhood like Ghweytarieh, they didn't have a two-hundred-square-metre pool. No, we didn't have anything, so we didn't even deserve kindness. You had to discard us, ignore us."

His father had his head down, he was shredding a piece of bread, rolling the little morsels. Siavash was talking loud, his voice was breaking, he was red and trembling, the mug in his hand shaking. The mug hit the saucer and rattled.

"Then when Parvin died you were happy. I could see it in your eyes, in mother's eyes, in Mojgan's and Mehran's. You thought that I was free then, that I would come back to your house of kindness and start all over again. Yes I returned, because I had no energy to work any more. I had no energy for anything any more, and you arranged for my trip. You rid yourself of me. You knew I was wasted. If I stayed, I would be destroyed, just looking at your happy faces would make me nauseous. I had to leave. I had to run away. At least you understood that, maybe only because of this I still feel something for all of you. Otherwise . . . "

He became silent, a few minutes passed in restraint. The father had nothing to say. He knew that whatever he said would make Siavash even angrier. For the past four months his son had done all he could for him, taken him to so many places. He introduced him to the Iranians of his own age, gave him money to buy all he wanted; gifts for his wife, children and grandchildren. He took him to his Iranian friends' houses, he gave parties for him.

Susan came out of the bedroom, noticed the silence between father and son. She took a magazine from the coffee table and looked at Siavash, but Saivash's head was down, his father looked at her with no smile and didn't say anything. Susan left the living room. The old man got up and poured tea for himself.

"Would you like some tea?"

Siavash shook his head, no.

His father sat at the table, took a sip of his tea.

"Forget all that. What is done is done."

Siavash started yelling so loudly that Susan came out of the bedroom and stared at them from the hallway.

"Finished and done with. Yes for you, it is all finished. It never even started, for it was all . . . "

His voice caught in his throat. The old man was puzzled.

"I didn't say anything, you wanted it, we weren't guilty."

"You didn't accept her, she was my wife."

"Now she is dead and buried."

"She died because of you all, not for me."

"You are not alone now, you have a new love in your life."

"So what does this have to do with anything? I am talking about the past, the past is not dead for me. You didn't want to accept her."

"But we were right too. That woman was not good for you. You hadn't finished your studies yet."

"It was no business of yours that I hadn't finished my studies. I was married to her. I got married in the City Hall, for God's sake, not like Mehran and Mojgan with all those ceremonies and lavish parties. We got married without a ring! Without a bridal gown, without any dinner party, no family, no nothing, do you understand that?"

"So what now? Why are you talking about the past? Why are you talking about ten or eleven years ago? You were nineteen years old, you fell in love with a twenty-five-year-old servant girl. What was our fault in that?"

"She wasn't twenty-five. Parvin was only two years older than me, two years, not five. And even if she was five years older, it wouldn't have mattered, no it didn't matter. I loved her and you didn't want to accept her."

"Well, now what can I do so you can forget."

"So I can forget? Why should I forget?"

The old man got up and went to the window. Siavash talked louder.

"All these years I was thinking about it. If you had accepted her, she wouldn't be dead now."

His father returned and looked at him. "But it wasn't our fault that she died, it was nobody's fault."

"You think you are not, but you and mother, you are all guilty. You could have helped us. Parvin died because the doctors were late. She died in a public hospital. If only . . . "

"But you weren't talking to us then. We didn't even know she was pregnant."

"Yes, I wasn't talking to you, because you had shunned her, you wouldn't answer her hello."

The father started screaming: "So why did you bring me here then? You wanted to tell me this? You could have written it all in a letter, what do you want to prove with this talk?"

"That you ruined my life."

"I don't see any ruin in your life. You got on with your studies, you have your job, you are not in bad shape either. You have fun with anybody you feel like, and you don't intend to marry either. You don't want to accept any responsibilities."

"This is not an excuse for you not to admit your guilt," Siavash screamed.

Susan got out of the room again, stood in the hallway looking at them. They became silent. She returned to the bedroom.

*

The father pushed his two heavy suitcases forward and showed his ticket and passport to the airline officer. The woman looked at his papers and gave them back to him. The suitcases were given to another officer. They had two hours before the airplane took off. They walked around inside the airport. Siavash suggested that they sit in a bar. Siavash ordered whiskey for his father and himself. His father drank a sip and smiled at him.

"Are you happy that you are leaving?"

His eyes were dancing happily but tears gathered in his eyes.

"I am worried about you."

"Why worry? You said it yourself, I have a good life."

"I wish you hadn't dumped Susan, she was a nice girl."

"What was so good about her?"

"She was educated, pretty, she was kind, and she loved you."

"I loved Parvin too."

"Don't start again."

Siavash took another sip. His cheekbones were flushed. He didn't know if it was alcohol or anger. He pressed his lips together.

"Forget it," his father said.

He was begging and asking for forgiveness.

Siavash looked at his father's eyes, but it seemed as if he couldn't see them. His father was uncomfortable.

"I don't forgive you."

The old man stared at the glasses on the table.

"You can not change the past, you'd better forget."

"But I don't forgive you," Siavash said bitterly.

He felt calm, while his father looked at him silently. For a few seconds their eyes met again. Siavash saw a strangeness in his father's eyes, some kind of coldness and indifference, as if saying, I don't forgive you either. You weren't a good son to me either.

But he said instead, "We'd better leave, it's getting late."

Saivash followed him out of the bar. They went to the transit doors together. They hugged each other. His father was crying and couldn't talk, Siavash was empty. He had said all that was in his heart. In the past few months he wanted to say so many things but he didn't. His father wanted to say something too, but he was quiet. They waved their arms as if they were strangers, and the old man disappeared.

Siavash stood for a minute looking at the closed doors, then a young couple holding their child opened the door and went inside. There was a long corridor behind the door, nobody was in there. Siavash left. The airport was filled with people of all races; women, men of all ages, their suitcases on top of carts, pushing them from one direction to another. But something had changed. There was a dead silence on their faces. The advertising panels and the TV screens with the announcements of arrivals and departures seemed empty and meaningless.

He sat on a bench. A black woman was sitting beside him with her newborn child asleep in her arms. Siavash stretched his legs. He sighed. He couldn't think or feel any more. He remembered his father's face when he had told him that he wouldn't forgive them. His words echoed in his head a few times. His father's face started to fade. He was so far away that Siavash couldn't remember him any more. When he looked again the woman beside him was gone. The area had emptied. He remembered his apartment and the empty place of his father. His loneliness was getting bigger and deeper. He tried to remember Parvin. She had run away from his memory. His father had taken her image away with him.

When he stood up, his face was covered with tears. He wiped his eyes hurriedly and left the airport. The night was spreading all over the city.

A Hand in the Cradle and a Foot in the Grave

Aqdas placed the tray of Persian tea glasses with their little saucers on the kitchen table. Akram stood next to the sink, water streaming over her hands onto the dishes.

"Put them here."

"No, these I'll wash. You're tired out."

"I'm not tired. Put them right here. Bring whatever else there is and I'll wash it. It's already getting dark out."

"You won't stay here tonight?"

"No, I've got to go. Haj Aqu and Mohsen are all alone. If I'm not there, they'll leave the house in the morning without any breakfast."

Aqdas set the tray of tea glasses next to her sister and left the kitchen. She brought back a few ashtrays along with a plate of half-eaten halva. The water streamed out of the faucet. Outside the window it was now completely dark.

Akram looked over her shoulder at Aqdas and asked, "There's no more?"

"No." Aqdas emptied the ashtrays in the garbage.

"What are they doing?"

"Sitting there."

"Aren't they talking?"

"Not much. Abdollah doesn't quite speak the same way anymore . . .

I don't know, have you noticed? Since he got here yesterday, he's hardly opened his mouth to say a word. I tried a few times to get him talking. A couple times he said some things that didn't make any sense. He kept saying, "Sorry."[1] What in the world does Sari have to do with Tehran! Do you suppose he's lost his bearings?"

Akram reached out to take the ashtrays. Casting a glance at the plate of halva, she said, "Put that back in the serving dish and give me the plate so I can wash it."

Aqdas took out the large bowl of halva, now half empty, from the refrigerator and scraped the halva off the plate into a corner of the bowl. With her finger, she put a dollop of halva into her mouth.

"This halva turned out marvelous. God rest her soul! She used to make a wonderful halva herself."

She gave Akram the plate, sat down on a chair and stared out the window into the darkness. She took out a cigarette and lit it up. She drew the smoke into her lungs.

Akram turned around and looked at her. "Poor thing, she died so young. It wasn't time for her to go yet."

"She's gone and left us to deal with all the headache. How will the poor professor manage, now?'

Akram put the last plate, still dripping with water, into the plastic dish rack next to the sink. She held the sponge under the water faucet and wrung it out in her hands. She wiped it over the rim of the sink and the edges of the counter and placed it back in the little dish at the side of the sink. Then she washed her hands under the faucet. Aqdas took a second puff on her cigarette, inhaling deeply. As she let it out, Akram turned off the water and dried her hands with a towel. She sat down on a chair and quickly lit a cigarette. "I was thinking about the Professor all afternoon. What about his work? He can't manage without a wife. In this big house . . . he's not even retired, at least then he'd be at home and could look after everything himself. After all, it's not much work to take care of just one person."

Aqdas shifted her gaze from the window to her sister. Aqdas had set down her cigarette on the ashtray and she watched the thick smoke emerge from her sister's thin lips. "What do you mean it's not much work! A big house like this? The professor has to go to work in the morning and doesn't get home until evening. Even at home he's busy with work, as you can see. He has to correct his students' homework. Poor Masumeh! Don't you remember how she always had her hand to her heart?"

"She died so young! The poor thing was barely forty-eight."

"And to think of it! Remember how Mother, God rest her soul, used to say that when they had gone to ask for Masumeh's hand in marriage, her family had complained that the groom was too old?"

"Too old? What nonsense. How old could he have been, anyway?"

"Thirty-five. But then, Mausmeh had not yet turned eighteen. Poor thing, life wore her out so soon."

"It was cancer that made her old. In these last couple years she aged twenty years."

"Damn cancer! She should have lived much longer. She held her husband together."

"You see, sister dear! When I used to tell her she should have more kids, you all mocked me. She gave birth to two boys and then bolted the door."

"The Professor didn't want more kids. He told me so himself. But Masumeh, well, she wanted a girl. The last few weeks, when she was bedridden and couldn't even go to the bathroom, she kept saying that if she had a daughter, she wouldn't be forced to have a stranger take care of her. Once I helped sit her on a bedpan. Poor thing; it was embarrassing for her."

Akram took a deep drag on her cigarette. "What are we going to do now? I've go to go. Anyway, what good is a daughter? I've got one of my own. She just up and left. I mean, she had to follow wherever her husband and kids went. You give birth to a daughter, she belongs to others. Give birth to a son, he belongs to others. Children are just not faithful."

"Well sis, as long as they are healthy. You shouldn't hope for anything more. If you send them abroad, you lose them too. Take

Abdollah. How poor Masumeh had her hopes set on seeing her sons! And as for the other one, Mahmud never even came at all."

"He must have been unable to make it. These days travel is no joking matter."

"They say he's not amounted to much; as for this one, he's dazed and confused. Have you listened to him talk? He gets some words all mixed up and you can't understand him. I don't know what 'excuse' is supposed to mean."

"Listen, sis, I have to go." Akram looked at her watch. "But before I go, I have something to tell you; think it over. It occurred to me today, while Khadijeh was here. What do you think about having Khadijeh's daughter come here?"

"I don't understand what you mean."

"I mean Golnaz. Khadijeh's older daughter. Khadijeh herself wouldn't mind a place for her daughter with a family she can trust. She is really good with sweeping, cleaning and washing. Not so bad looking, either." Akram paused momentarily, and a faint smile formed on her lips. She continued, "We'll quietly marry her to the Professor so their relationship won't be illicit."[2]

Aqdas looked dubiously at her sister and fell to thinking.

"What do you think?" asked Akram. "We cannot come here every day, make lunch and dinner for the Professor and look after a house as big as this. On the other hand, we cannot just abandon him and pray that everything, turns out all right. What would people say? He's our brother, he's family. And as you know, men just haven't a clue. He hasn't dirtied his fingers even once in his life. He doesn't know how to take care of himself. He might do something to himself one day, like pour rat poison in his food instead of salt by mistake. Then we'd have to answer to him and God for the rest of our lives."

Aqdas was lost in thought. After a while, she fixed a steady gaze on her sister and asked, "You mean Khadijeh would be willing to marry off Golnaz to the Professor?"

"Why wouldn't she? She should thank her lucky stars. The girl's missing a few marbles, you know. So far nobody has come asking for her. You know how maids and laundry women are, they marry off their daughters young. Khadijeh's second girl is already spoken for. Her uncle's boy has come to Tehran from the villages and is working in a factory. It looks as if they'll be married in the summer."

"Yes, sister, but be reasonable. How can you marry off a half-witted girl? Do you think the Professor would go for it?"

"I'll fix it, he'll agree. You don't know men. The Professor always had an eye for women. Don't you remember how Masumeh quarreled with him several times and went off to her father's house? All because of the Professor's fooling around."

"But with a servant girl?"

"Don't worry about it. I'll take care of it. The thing is that I can't be coming here every day and night all by myself. You know what kind of man Haj Aqu is—jealous and mean. He imagines I've got a secret rendezvous set up here. He can't bear to see me lift my fingers even for own brother and sister. You'd think I was his slave, body and soul. What can I do? I can't fight with him all my life, after all. Besides as God and Prophet have said, a woman must serve her husband. Well, a body's brother has a claim on her, too. I have to figure out some way to work this out, or people will talk. So what do you think?"

"I just don't know. If you think it will work, well, go ahead and do it. First of all, you've got to get the Professor to go along with it. The Professor is no corner grocer, you know. He's been respected all his life, he teaches in the University. Boys and girls study under his direction. Now, how about if you tell him to get involved with one of his female students? Girls are always falling in love with their teachers. Why, I myself fell in love with my religious studies teacher when I was in the seventh grade."

"Mr Fotuhi?"

"Yeah."

"You have a lousy taste!"

"Well, I was just a kid, I didn't know any better."

"But you're lucky your husband is not like Mr Fotuhi, or else—"

"Or else what? He was like Mr Fotuhi. I just had to put up with him. There's no getting around it."

Akram got up. She looked out the window of the kitchen. The house light was on. "I'm going to go call Haj Aqu and have him come get me. There's no transportation at this time of night."

When she came back, Aqdas had poured two glasses of tea and put them on the tray. "Who are those for?"

"For Abdollah and the Professor."

"Pour one for me, too."

Aqdas poured one tea, set it in front of her sister and went into the next room. When she came back Akram asked, "What were they doing?"

"The Professor is sitting at his desk leafing through a pile of papers and Abdollah was reading a book."

"Shall we go in the other room and sit with them for a while?"

"What for? They don't talk with us," said Aqdas. "Do you really think the plan will work?"

"What plan?"

"What you were saying just now—marrying Khadijeh's girl to the Professor."

"And why not? It's the only way."

"And if Golnaz should get pregnant, what then?"

Akram pondered the matter. She got up and poured herself another tea. She held the hot tea to her lips and took a sip. "Do you want tea?" she asked.

"No."

"I hadn't thought of that. We have to direct her to be careful. . ."

"What do you mean, direct? You can't follow her into the bed between the sheets! What if she feels like having kids. Once the Professor is her legal husband? She must want kids. Khadijeh probably wouldn't mind to have a grandchild by the Professor, either. In the end some of his money and estate would go to her."

"I hadn't thought of that. No ringing the bell with a foot in the grave; no, she mustn't get pregnant."

"You should have to fix it before the marriage. How would it be if we take her to a doctor and have her tubes tied?"

"How? You can't hand over a virgin girl to a midwife. So, you see, it's not as easy as you think."

"We have to have a talk with the Professor. He must be made to understand to take precautions. The Professor is not terribly fond of kids. As you know, Masumeh only had two kids."

"And what if one day the girl gets pregnant by somebody else? After all, a seventeen- or eighteen-year-old girl is not going to be satisfied with a sixty-five-year-old man. What if it happens she gets pregnant, huh? What's more, you say she's not got all her marbles. What would people say? Don't you think it will make things worse?"

"How should I know? Anyway, we have to think of something. Running the Professor's household is too big job for you and me."

"It seems to me you have to plant the notion in the Professor's head for him to go and find a girl for himself. One of his students. If they work something out on their own, there would be no headache for us to deal with."

"Nonsense, sis. An educated girl would never marry a sixty-five-year-old man."

"Who says she wouldn't? Haven't you heard about Dr Farudi? He's just about the same age as our Professor? He's taken a twenty-year-old girl as his wife."

"Really? When?"

"Haven't you heard? His first wife isn't speaking to him and has gotten up and left."

"Mahin Khanum? With four kids?"

"Yeah. The kids are grown up. It seems the Doctor falls in love with one of his patients, or one of his patients with him. I don't know . . . And then he secretly takes her as a sigheh. Then it happens that the girl gets pregnant. She must deliver any day now. The Doctor has legally married her."

"Where did you hear all this?"

"I heard it just today. It's becoming a real scandal. Parvin Khanum was telling me about it."

"The poor woman. What will she do now?"

"I told you, she stopped speaking to him and has gone to her family in Mashhad. I think she wants to get a divorce."

Akram got up and went to the window. "I don't know what's keeping him. You can't leave these damn men alone for even one night. Right away they start chasing after women."

Aqdas laughed and said, "You're the one who's going to the side of your husband. You'll go and leave me here all alone."

"You, your husband is not a raffish bastard."

"How would you know? As the saying goes, Have no fear of men who bark and riot; beware the one who acts all calm and quiet."

The sound of car brakes made her get up. "He's here; I'm going. You go talk to the Professor. Get him to go along with the plan."

"Have you thought the thing through to the end?"

"We'll think about that later."

"But, sister, at least wait until the poor woman is cold in her grave."

"Why worry about the poor woman's corpse? You have to think about the living."

NOTE

1. Sory is a city in north of Tehran, and has the same sound as "sorry" in English.

2. According to Islam, a man and woman who are not a close family can't live together in the same house.

The Last Anniversary

It was one of June's beautiful days, the day he saw her for the first time. Sitting on a chair on the verandah, as he did all day when the weather was fine, sipping from a cup of tea, he had absentmindedly sunk into his melancholy daydreams. The very pleasant weather, the silence of the trees, the bird's random songs far away or close by, the bright slanting sunshine, the house surrounded by deep silence and happiness, enthralled him for hours. And when he recovered his consciousness, he was surprised and wondered what he had been dreaming about.

It was a bird's song that he paid attention to, as if it had woken him up. Close to him, on the tree in the front yard, a bird was singing clearly—a sad, sharp song evoking his memories. He searched through the branches but couldn't find the bird. Only its song echoed in the surrounding silence. Tired from looking for the bird, he eyed the other side of the street and saw a woman sitting on a bench, knitting. At first he thought it was an illusion. He blinked a few times and watched carefully. The bench seemed unusual to him there, because the neighborhood had big houses with the vast backyards and front yards with rocking chairs, benches, and fancy swings. In the two and half years he had been living in the house, people usually passed the street by car. Nobody sat on the bench.

He noticed the woman but he couldn't see what she was knitting from that distance. Occasionally she lifted her eyes and looked around.

He forgot about the bird's song, and when he remembered it again he couldn't hear it any more, but from perhaps a few houses away another bird sang languidly. Then there was silence again, not even a breeze whispered among the leaves. The sun's rays slanted further and brightness faded.

He lifted his cup. It was empty. He couldn't remember when he had finished his tea. He would have liked to have more, but he didn't want to move. Staring at the woman, he wondered if he had seen her before. Her hands moving harmonically, her head tilted to the left with a slight bow in her back, she reminded him of his own wife. He felt a deep, sharp sorrow. It was more than two years ago that he had lost her, far from himself. She had gone to be with her younger son's children. The son had been executed for political offenses and his wife was working. This daughter-in-law needed someone to take care of her children. So his wife went back home and didn't return.

They had come here together to see their elder son who was a doctor and had a happy life with his wife—a dentist—and two young healthy beautiful daughters. They came to this country after a long separation from the elder son and saw their grandchildren for the first time. Those six months were enjoyable. The son applied for their immigration papers, they could stay as long as they liked. But his wife couldn't stand to be far from her other grandchildren, who had lost their father and were still very young. So she left him here and returned. He felt jealous of his grandchildren but he said nothing. He knew that when she decided to do something, nobody could stop her.

After she left, life was not easy with his son's family. There were always small conflicts between him and his daughter-in-law or his grandchildren. In telephone conversations with his wife he begged her to come back and always received the same answer, "I will." He decided to live alone by himself, to persuade his wife to come back. His son wanted rent an apartment for him, but he didn't like those high, huge buildings that reminded him of beehives. So they lodged him in a house belonging to a family his age.

The house was big—located in a rich, quiet and beautiful neighborhood. The man liked the house, the street, the trees and the people who, whenever they met him walking in the empty streets, greeted him kindly and exchanged a few words with him that he barely understood.

Six months after his wife left, his daughter-in-law called him and informed him that his wife had had a stroke. He couldn't believe it. His son took him to his house to console him. He called home everyday but nobody answered. He called during the day when his son and his daughter-in-law were at work and his grandchildren were at school. Finally, he heard a voice on the phone that he didn't recognize. She told him she was his wife's sister and sobbed—like a person sobbing over a death. She informed him of his wife's death but he couldn't believe it.

Sometimes the man, sitting on the verandah, staring at nowhere, fully occupied with his melancholy daydreams, convinced himself that his wife hadn't died yet. A faint illusion filled his mind that she was back there and waiting for her immigration papers in order to come here. When he saw the man and the woman in the house and how happy they were together, when they invited him for their fiftieth anniversary, he was sorry he never remembered his own anniversary with his wife, who was kind and gentle and never raised her voice. He was surprised that he never noticed how good she was to him, and how she took care of him. He wished he could go back home and see her sitting beside the fireplace in the winter, knitting or reading a book. He never asked what she was knitting or what book she was reading.

The sunset spread all over as he stared at the woman, who stopped knitting. She stood up and, without looking around, left the bench and walked away. She walked to the left, towards the sunset, and turned left into a narrow alley connected to a small grove with trees woven into each other, and disappeared.

The summer was not over yet, but the days with fine weather had grown fewer. The leaves on the trees turned red, yellow, brown and into a mix of colours. The sky was more blue and pure, but some days were gray and covered with clouds. The cool breeze turned to chill wind that made him shiver when he sat on the verandah. But he took a coat or sweater and sat on a chair and waited for the woman. She had always the same dress and knitted with a gray thread. The man didn't talk to anybody about her. He knew that nobody would believe him, nobody would see her. He feared that if he talked about her, they would disturb her and she might not come any more. He wanted to talk to her himself, but didn't know when to. He didn't have the courage. Whenever he felt very strongly the desire to talk to the woman, he remembered his own wife. He thought of her loyalty and couldn't decide.

His wife seemed innocent as a victim of death. When he accepted that she was dead and wouldn't come back, he felt a deep sorrow, was pushed into a deep melancholy. He wished that the woman on the bench were his wife or at least his wife's shadow or soul coming to see him. These feelings were sweet and evoked in him more dreams. Now he was dreaming about their wedding anniversary. A very luxurious anniversary with many people invited, a big cake, and beautiful gifts for her. He saw the woman sitting quietly, knitting or staring into nowhere. He sank into his own dreams, until darkness covered him and the cool breeze of the end of summer made him shiver. He looked at the bench—the woman had gone. He stood up. There was a pain in his muscles and his heart. A gloomy shadow covered his mind. He went into his room, turned the TV on which his son had bought for his eighty-first birthday. The faces, the words, the scenes were unfamiliar and weird to him. He didn't understand what was going on, what they were talking about, what they were laughing at, what they were crying about. He lay down on the bed. The program ended, a commercial was shown, then another program came up. He just wanted a voice in the room. He remembered that when he was living with his wife, she was usually silent. They talked occasionally. It seemed they had nothing to talk about. But she was there. She always answered his questions—even he didn't answer her always, she who was kind, gentle and quiet. He was never alone, and if he was, he was sure she would return home. And now he didn't know if she would. Sometimes he dreamed she would return. He dreamed about the woman on the bench. He never asked himself who she was, where she was coming from. He was sure she came because of him, and this certainty made him feel better. The sorrow faded in him. Feeling hungry, he went to the kitchen to eat the food the landlady had left in his fridge. He warmed it in the microwave, and sitting by the table he ate his food. Whenever the man or the woman came to the kitchen, he smiled at them absentmindedly, talked to them using the few words he had learned, and again sank into his dreams.

Summer turned to autumn. Fallen leaves cracked under his feet. The wind howled among trees and in crevices in the windows. It was not possible to sit on the verandah any more. Whenever he sat there, someone advised him to go in, or the cold weather sent him in. He put a chair at the window in his room and sat on it, stared at the bench, waited for the woman to come.

When he saw her, covered in a heavy coat, with a black scarf, sitting there knitting, a stream of joy flew through his heart. He was sure she had come for his sake. He decided to talk to her. Every night when he went to bed, he thought about his decision and was certain that the next time he saw her he would talk to her.

Fall was almost over. The first snow fell before it was really winter. The street was covered with snow and ice. Winds were gusting, the weather grew colder. The man was waiting and thinking about the next spring. A heavy snow fell, everywhere was completely white. The bare trees were covered by snow, and the branches looked full of white blooms. At five o'clock, darkness spread everywhere. Snow shone under the street's light. The neighborhood was so quiet that he imagined that life had vanished from the earth. Waiting by the window, he felt lost, sad, and wished for death. When he saw the woman, sitting on the bench, he didn't know when she had come. Perhaps he had lost track in his gloomy dreams, she appeared and sat on the bench and now she was there—in a heavy coat, scarf, and boots—knitting. Still knitting.

The man shivered with joy. He remembered his decision. "I should talk to her."

He put on his coat, his hat, his scarf, his boots, his gloves, to leave the house. The woman in the house asked him where he was going, in that terrible weather. Ignoring her question, he left the house. Enthusiastic to talk to the woman, he went towards her. She got up and walked away. She walked the same direction that she had walked all those times. He followed her through the small grove. The trees were like white ghosts. The wind howled through the icy branches. The woman looked back and smiled at him. A strong feeling of joy warmed him. He walked faster to reach her.

A Blind Love

Father opens the letter and reads it. Mr Falahati is sitting on the other side of the desk. He is a middle-aged man who called me and introduced himself as Parviz's lawyer, and asked me to come and see him here.

"I'll come with you, too," Father said.

Father reads the letter. I don't watch him. Mr Falahati looks at me once in a while and at Father. Either the letter is long or father reads it slowly. He looks up from the letter, looks preoccupied with what he's already read. A faint smile is on his face. He says nothing.

Mr Falahati says, " Do you understand?"

Father regains himself, he looks at me, tongue-tied, astonishment and joy in his face.

"What does it say, Father?" I ask. Father says nothing.

Mr Falahati says, "Why don't you tell her. Tell her the truth."

I look at father. He's quiet, happy but stunned.

Mr Falahati says, " Mr Parviz Basharti has left all his properties to you."

"To me?"

The whole the city knows about it. All my classmates, all my teachers. I'm infamous. Nasrin says, "Why infamous? He loves you. A blind love. Why don't you marry him?"

I don't love him. I hate his short height, his big head, his rude looks and his big mouth. I hate his cheeky behavior.

"You love someone else?"

Yes, I love someone else. But I don't talk about him to anyone. We walk through deserted alleys, Goodarz holding my hand. An intoxicating stream passes through my veins. I talk nonstop. In the sunset we stand under a big plane tree. We should part. I've left my house to study with my friend. I'm notorious according to everyone. Goodarz looks at me. I like his eyes; they are the colour of ashes. There's always sadness in them. As if they hide an inaccessible love.

"Parviz has spread a rumour everywhere that you've replied to his love."

"Me? He's wrong. I want to marry you."

"Me?"

"Yes, you."

He holds my hand. Power surges in me. I hug him and kiss him. He looks at me, stunned, and then he presses me to him, answering me with a long kiss. We have made our promise.

Father says, "Well, my daughter."

Happiness and joy erupts from his eyes.

"I congratulate you, " Mr Falahati says. "The late Mr Basharati . . ."

When I come out of the school, he's there. Nasrin says goodbye to me and leaves. Parviz walks shoulder to shoulder with me. Ignoring him, I continue on my way.

He says, "I love you. I love you very much. Why don't you answer me?"

"Leave me alone," I say.

"I won't leave you alone, " he persists, "until I get you, you'll see. You're mine."

"You just waste your time, " I tell him. "You may get me when I'm dead."

"You'll see," he says.

"If I see you one more time in my way, I'll report you to the police."

"Report to all the constables in the city, I won't leave you alone. "

A car brakes in front of me. It is the colour of a green lawn and shines. I am about to cross the street, having checked both directions. Carrying my son Rameen has made me tired. I'm coming home from a doctor's office. I curse myself, why didn't I bring his stroller. I wish I could get a cab. But just two blocks remain to my home. A man appears before me. Parviz. He is the same short man, but has gained weight. He seems older. There are white hairs on his head. He looks at me. There's no rudeness in his face, a sadness shadows him.

"Don't you remember me?"

I'm shocked. I feel the heaviness of Rameen's body. The child has put his head on my shoulder and is asleep.

"I would like to come to your house and offer my condolence."

There are tears in my eyes. I say thank you quietly

"Will you let me give you a ride?"

I shake my head and continue on my way.

Father says, "My daughter, think better, he's not a bad man."

Mother says, "He loves you. Since he has come back after so many years, it's clear that he loves you."

Nasrin says, "What a love! After so many years, still flaming. What's the matter with you? Happiness is flying over your head and you don't want it."

"After the final exams we will get married and then we will go to Fesham."[1]

He leaves the letter in my hand and walks away. He doesn't block my way anymore. He stands farther and stares at me. There's a rumour that he tried to commit suicide and was rescued. His letter is full of begging and cursing. He wishes me misfortune and Goodarz death.

I tear the letter up and throw it away. I don't talk about it to Goodarz. Nasrin says, "You broke his heart, you will pay for it."

"I don't owe him anything. I don't love him. I can't help it."

A Blind Love

The day after our wedding we go to Fesham. The sunshine in the month of Khordad is intoxicating. The earth breathes happily. The sky in the mountain tops is a pure blue. The river flows quietly. We get up early in the morning and go hiking. There's love in our veins instead of blood. Goodarz reads me poetry and I become drunk with his voice and his poems.

Maziar opens the door. I'm sitting in the living room. Rameen is sleeping on my lap. I can't stand up.

"It's a man at the door," Maziar says

"Ask him his name."

I hear his voice, "Parviz."

Maziar returns. I say, "Tell him, my mother isn't at home."

Maziar goes to the door. Parviz is standing in the doorway. I cover my leg with my skirt. I'm dressed in black. My hair is undone. He doesn't look away from me.

"I've come to talk to you. In fact I wanted to offer my sympathy."

I leave Rameen on the floor. He wakes up. I sit on a sofa, Parviz too. I didn't invite him to sit. I can't avoid crying. Rameen too is crying. I take the child in my arms. Maziar and Afshin stand beside me. Maziar caresses my hair, as Goodarz did when he was with me.

"Don't cry, Maman."

I wipe my tears. Parviz gets up and gives me the box of Kleenex. Maziar pulls one out and gives it to me. I say to Maziar, "Go and make milk for the baby." Rameen is crying. Parviz takes the baby from me and walks in the living room. The child looks at him with astonishment. Maybe he sees the shadow of his father on him. Maziar comes back with a baby bottle of milk. He's wondering if he should give the bottle to Parviz or to me. I take the bottle from him. I want to take the baby from Parviz too, but I can't move. Tears don't leave me. I see Goodarz. We are sitting on a mountain slope. Moonlight is everywhere. Goodaraz reads poetry. His low vibrant voice is like the spring rain:

"Moonlight's flowing

a worm is glowing
not a breath to break slumber in the eye
and yet
the thought of this sleeping bunch
breaks sleep in my watery eyes."[2]

I want to get up and go to the bedroom. I don't have the strength.
I'm tired. Sobbing shakes my body. Parviz sits beside me. Maziar and
Afshin look at me in silence, their eyes full of sadness.
"Please, don't cry."
He puts his hand on my shoulder. A shiver runs under my skin.
His letter is full of curses. He has wished death for Goodarz and
misery for me.
I get up and stay farther away. I tell Maziar to take the baby from
him. He's shocked. He gives the baby to Maziar. I take the baby from
Maziar, put the bottle in his mouth and go to my bedroom. I leave the
baby in his cradle. I'm waiting for Parviz to leave. I've lost the cour-
age of those years. He's no longer the rude and noisy young man.
He's talking with Maziar and Afshin.

I'm walking in Pahlavi Street hand in hand with Goodarz. I see
Parviz standing on the pavement, his hair disheveled.
"Your restive lover doesn't leave you alone," Goodarz says
"He gets nothing."
We pass by him. I feel his look following me.
"He's not a bad man, " Father says. "After so many years . . . "
"A blind love," Nasrin says, "he surely loves you."
"Think about your children," Mother says, "it won't be easy with a
teaching income."
"An apartment building," Father says, "and thousands of square
meters of land and a construction company."
"His wealth is without measure," Mother says.
I come back from work. I have put a black dress on. I don't pluck my
eyebrow. I have a black scarf on my head. I see myself in a shop's

mirror. I've become old, suddenly old. There's a wrinkle between my eyebrows. My eyes have lost their glow. My hands have become old.

"Because of washing so many clothes."

"My washing machine is broken."

He's standing by the alley. His green car is parked close by. I saw his car from a distance. I know he's there.

"If you let me, I'll have few words with you."

"What words? My children are alone at home."

"I know, your mother is with them. It doesn't take too long. I talked to your mother."

"What about?"

"Please, just a few minutes."

"Think about it well," Goodarz says. "He has a decent life. His father is wealthy. He's an engineer too. He has a construction company. Me . . . a poor teacher. You'll have to get along with poverty."

I don't care about his talk. I don't want to care. I say, "Love doesn't know poverty."

"It's not possible to live just with love. An empty stomach doesn't know love."

"But I'll work too. I'll get a job as a teacher."

"Even with the salaries of two teachers, life still would be hard."

"We would have our love, instead,"

"And then, when we have children, it won't be easy."

"With love life can be easier."

"Didn't I tell you, didn't I tell you, you wouldn't be happy with love."

"No, don't say anything. I'm happy."

"After me. Didn't I tell you?"

"After you, life means nothing. You'll always be, always. "

"With this illness, with this leukemia?"

I swallow my lump. Goodarz is slowly melting. Goodarz is lost in darkness. In less than six mouths he is lost like a bird in the vastness of the sky. He's gone. I can't find him anywhere; at home or in the street. He exists only in my dreams.

"I told you, don't make a mistake. Parviz has everything. He wouldn't leave you with nothing even after his death."

"But I loved you. And always I'll love you."

"But I'm going to perish."

"Don't talk like that. You'll always be. You'll be in Maziar, Afshin and Rameen. You'll always be with me."

"I've talked to your mother. She accepts it. She said you have a hard time."

"I don't understand what you mean."

" I . . . How do I say it? I still . . . "

I look at him. There's no a sign of that Parviz in him. He's solemn and aged. His bluster is gone.

"You're a married man. Do you have any children?"

"No, fortunately. I didn't want to have any children. The marriage isn't anything more than a convention. "

"What do you mean?"

"I don't love my wife. I'll divorce her, in fact . . . "

"You would divorce her. So simple?"

"I love you. You know that I love you. All these years, do you remember?"

I look at him. I see the same Parviz in him.

"I'll get you out of his hands. If I have to wait for a hundred years I'll get you out of his hands. I won't be afraid even of death."

"I told you, love is blind. Be rational."

"My blind love just sees you."

I tell him roughly, "What do you mean?"

"What do I mean? You should understand what I mean."

I look at my black dress. It's eight months since Goodarz's death. I saw him coming from the end of the street. Death is clear in his pale complexion. Leukemia has drained his strength, but he's not fallen yet.

"Forgive me. I wasn't a good man for you. I'll abandon you to the streets, with three small children."

"Don't say that. These are you. Each one has part of you. Please be quiet."

"If I say so you should accept it."

"If you just give me a few minutes, I'll talk to you in a few words."

"What about?"

"I still love you."

"Well?"

"Do you agree . . . "

"You have a wife."

" I'll divorce her."

"I don't understand."

"Think better of it, " Mother says, "life isn't easy with a teacher's salary, with three children, without a house, without a car, it's not a joke."

Mother is angry with me.

"He wants to divorce his wife so that I may marry him."

"He'll be a father for your sons."

"They already have a father."

"They don't. Their father is dead."

"Their father is alive in them."

"You are lucky with your dreams. Open your eyes and look at yourself. You've grown ten years older in the last eight months."

"I don't want to be young any more."

"Just let me be a father for your sons."

"Father . . . "

"Yes, I know you don't love me and you never will. I understand that you still . . . "

"You wished him death."

"It was because of youth and stupidity."

"And he died."

"He didn't die because of my wish."

"And he died."

"Please accept my condolences."

"You wished him death."

"And now if you permit me, I'll be a good father for your children."

"My children don't need a father."

"I'll get you away from him, I'll wait for a hundred years to get you out of his hands."

Nasrin says, "Have you heard?'

"What?"

"Parviz Basharati got married to a wealthy girl."

"What do you say, " my father says, "all the wealth of Mr Basharati . . . "

"I wasn't a good companion for you, I'll leave you in the streets . . . "

"Don't say that. Our lives have been as long as eternity. I'll have all those moments . . . "

"You'll have a hard time. If there is good man . . . "

"No."

I close his eyes with my own hands. As he dies, his last breath is the most relaxed one. He is staring at me and breathes the last one, after me . . .

I put my head on his chest. It's still. My sobbing shocks everyone. It's dawn. The spring breeze passes over his body.

"Spring has a strange feeling. Spring means love."

"It was in spring when I saw you and fell in love with you."

It's spring when I bury him.

"When I heard, I was so sorry."

"You wished him dead."

"It was because of youth. I was in love with you. A blind love. I'm still in love with you."

I go my way. He stays and watches me.

"Think about everything," Father says.

I say, "Goodarz isn't dead. I see him in my dreams every night."

"It's not necessary to marry him tomorrow. A year later, two years later. But don't run him off. He's heartbroken."

"But he has a wife."

"He doesn't love his wife. He has told me about everything. He was forced to marry."

"With a wealthy girl."

"There is a husband for that girl."

"You're still young, " Mother says, "not thirty years old yet. With three children. Do you think it's easy? They will grow up and leave you. It's not easy to control children without a father."

"Their father is, " I say, "their father is in them. I feel him, they too."

"Be rational, my dear daughter," Father says, "you were wrong even when you married Goodarz. But you were young. Goodarz was sick then."

"He was not. Goodarz was sick for less than one year. Goodarz was full of love."

"Love or anything else, he has gone and won't come back. You know that he won't come back."

"Goodarz is with me, he's with me everywhere."

"But he'll go. The soil brings forgetfulness."

It's drizzling. The street is covered with yellow leaves. I'm standing by the kitchen window watching the rain. Rameen stands beside me. Maziar and Afshin are at school. They should be back any moment. I'm waiting for them. When I see them in the street, I wave to them. Rameen wants me to pick him up. I can't. He's three years old, he's heavy. He's stuck to my legs. I pick him up, I'm tired of standing. The apartment in the afternoon is silent. I go to the living room. I stand in front of Goodarz's photo, show it to Rameen and say, "Baba."

"Baba?" he asks.

There's no recognition of his father in his voice. He doesn't remember his father and I want to remind him.

Goodarz is sitting on a cushion on the other side of living room, reading Shamloo.[3] I say, "Read it aloud."

"And my love is a cage, empty of bird—sad, bored."

His voice is lost in silence. I try to listen to the rest of the poem, I don't hear him.

"You still are the same stubborn girl, " Father says, " why don't you want him?"

I don't answer him. I see Parviz sometimes here and there. He knows that insisting is useless. I don't love him.

I look at gray eyes. What they say is not clear to me.

"Nothing. You like to dream."

"Why are you so sad?"

"It's not in my control."

"I love your sadness."

"My sadness is for you. After me . . . "

"Don't talk like that."

"I'm wondering why you don't love him," Nasrin says. "Isn't it said that a heart has connection with another heart?"

"I don't have a heart."

"He has divorced his wife. What more do you want?"

I don't know what I want. My house is getting colder. Mother brings me rice and oil. Father buys clothes for Afshin and Maziar. Nasrin buys a tricycle for Rameen. My teaching money runs out before the end of every month. I'm learning to type, so I can get another job.

"You're crazy. He is gone too."

I read the news in the newspaper. The condolence notices have filled *Keyhan* and *Etelaat*.[4] "The passing away of Parviz Basharati in a car accident."

My apartment is full of silence. I look at Goodarz's photo.
"I'm sorry. I'm so sorry. I abandoned you. If there's a good man . . ."
His voice fades into silence.
"Read me poetry."
"What poetry?"
"Read from Hafez."
"In the end our dwelling is the valley of silence
Now into the vault of the skies the shout and clamour are cast!"
I don't hear him.

"You see, " Nasrin says, " you did nothing until he too . . . "
"It wasn't my fault."
"I heard that he was drunk when he was driving. He had abandoned his job."
"How do you know that?"
"I heard it from someone who knew him."
"Don't believe it. People say many things."
"But he loved you."
"I didn't love him."

Mr Falahati says, "The lady should sign this paper and all the wealth of Mr Basharati will be transferred to her."
Father gives the papers to me. There's joy in his eyes.
The wealth of Mr Basharati . . .

Parviz is standing by the street. I see his car. His hair is disheveled. He comes towards me. I smell alcohol on him from a few meters away.
"Get out of my way."

"Marry him. He'll make a good life for you. You need a man."

"I don't."

My house is empty. I take Goodarz's photo from the wall. His voice has disappeared in me. My love is dead, it has gone to the earth.

"The soil brings forgetfulness," Mother says.

Father holds the letter out to me.

"Come on my daughter, sign it."

I get up and go out of the lawyer's office. I see Goodarz in the street.

"Crazy, you're still the same crazy lover."

"I'm not; not crazy, and not a lover."

NOTES

1. A suburb of Tehran for summer vacationers.

2. A poem by Nima Youshij, from *An Anthology of Modern Persian Poetry,* translated by Ahmad Karimi Hakkak, Westview Press, 1978.

3 Shamloo, a contemporary poet in Iran who died in 2000.

4 Two major newspaper in Iran.

Happiness in Five Definitions

It was Bahman who initiated the discussion about happiness. The night, the moonlight, the forest, the silence, the fire which flamed occasionally spreading a pleasant heat, the glory of nature, so rich and deep, might have been the reason why Bahman, who had been thinking about happiness for a long time, posed his question and raised a lot of discussion. But, also he was a person with questions, eager to know everybody's definition about of life, happiness. Bahman collected booklets and asked everyone their idea about everything. He had read and heard many definitions and still in any gathering he posed a question when something came to mind. They were sitting around a fire in a provincial camping area. Three tents in different colours and sizes close to each other, with the children asleep in them. Bahman hadn't married yet and didn't have any children. Perhaps because of that, he liked to busy himself posing questions to friends and companions, seeking answers on any aspect of life.

Hamed was always interested in Bahman's questions and definitions. He was the first person to volunteer an answer. Not only did Hamed consider himself a happy man, but also, others had no doubt that he deserved to be happy. He had a good education: a PhD in mathematics, which meant he had a perfectly logical conception of his life, no doubts, illusions or mirages. A PhD in mathematics meant he was a man of action with a good job, a good salary and most important, his job was secure. Many organizations which sought intelligence, looked to him. Hamed had a good wife—obedient, loyal, receptive and inferior to him. He had good children, both gifted and well nourished, showing no sign of problems in school. So, to many, Hamed deserved to be happy. And he was aware and proud of his happiness.

"What does happiness mean in your opinion?" Bahman asked.

Hamed had his answer ready. First, he looked around, to be sure of himself. The fire flamed again with the dry wood Bahman had added. "I wish you had posed a more complicated question," Hamed said, "happiness has a simple definition."

Abdolah, a man of defeated initiatives and bankrupt businesses, a man of fruitless works, a disappointed man of hard work that yielded no fruit, who liked to make fun of any serious job, who always had a sneer rather than a smile, looked at Hamed. Abdolah sometimes confused a sneer and a smile. He believed there was no seriousness in life. Everything looked like a comedy ever since he had been uprooted from his homeland and thrown far away. Serious matters had turned into jokes. Abdolah looked at Hamed and said, "The most simple definitions might be the most complex to explain. For example, aging, it's so simple, everybody can feel it everyday, fatigue in your body and wrinkles on your face in the mirror. This simple phenomenon relates to the whole universe. If you want to learn about it, you need to study the milky way and the black holes and solar system. Because the whole universe is aging with you."

Hamed was annoyed with Abdolah's habit of commenting on every single word coming out from everybody's mouth, especially Hamed's, who had been interrupted several times that day. He said impatiently, "I have nothing to do with the whole universe. I would like to give you a simple definition of happiness. Isn't that a clear answer?"

Homa admired Hamed silently, as she had done all her life, like a dog admiring her master even when he does nothing. She looked at Abdolah and was offended that he had interrupted Hamed again. She cursed Abdolah quietly. She believed Hamed was the most important person among men, and even more among men and women, because women were nonentities.

Hamed scrutinized all with a hurt look on his face, waiting for Bahman to insist on his answer. Bahman waited for Hamed's answer. Manijeh pushed the half-burned wood into the fire, with a vague smile on her face. She was a learned woman. Manijeh had many definitions for social and spiritual ideals. She was partly a philosophical thinker. She knew names of philosophers, and sometimes she mentioned them as if speaking in code. She preferred the talk of intellectual people and didn't let men consider her a woman of the kitchen and bed.

These men! she told herself, how happy they are with their own talking. Assume that you had a simple or a difficult, general or common definition of happiness. What then? You can't change anything with talk. Manijeh preferred to sing, rather than have such stupid discussions with men who just boasted to each other. A song by Marzieh was playing in her head. The moon watched them in silence. Manijeh imagined the moon had a sneer on her shiny round face as if she was making fun of their discussion. Happiness!

"Well, Mr Hamed,"said Bahman, "give us your simple definition of happiness in one sentence, not more."

"Yes, one sentence," Hamed said, "just one sentence. Happiness means to be pleased with one's own self."

The silence lasted only a few seconds. A piece of wood in the fire burst with a loud noise, and Abdolah's hysterical laughter burst into the silence of the forest, lake, moonlight, and tents, and the hidden animal and bird in dreamless sleep. They all looked at Abdolah, astounded. Nobody had said anything to laugh at. They waited for Abdolah to explain his laughter, but he became quiet. He stared at the flames spreading heat and light without caring about silence or laughter.

Ready to defend his idea, Hamed sneered at Abdolah and said, "Which part of my definition was funny?"

Abdolah turned from the fire to Hamed, surprised, saying, "Me? I didn't mean that. I didn't laugh at your idea. Tell the truth, I didn't hear what you said. I laughed at Bahman's question. Happiness!" And Abdolah burst into laughter again. The others laughed with him involuntarily, except Hamed, who was like a fighting cock ready to defend himself. Homa put her hand on his knees and pressed. Like a very loyal dog she had some words to say, but she was unable to utter them. She wanted to say, "Don't worry my dear, people are jealous." That was the sentence she had repeated many times in the past twelve years of their common lives. It was the only sentence she imagined would comfort Hamed in these situations.

"Is it possible to explain your idea?" Bahman said. "To be pleased with one's own self, how is that attained?"

Abdolah hid his laughter, pretended to be serious, as a student in a classroom, and said, "Can I explain it?"

Bahman glanced at Abdolah and then at Hamed and said, "If Hamed agrees, you can."

Manijeh was singing Marzieh's song in her head, enthralled with the beauty of the night, with the warmth of the fire and the breeze from the lake. She seemed to wake from a dream, abandoning the song in the middle, and with an indignation always present when she addressed Abdolah, said, "Why are you going to explain Hamed's answer? Hamed has a tongue and knowledge about everything and is qualified to speak about happiness. Did you forget that you always deny happiness?"

Abdolah felt betrayed, as he always did facing his wife. If his wife permitted him, he could explain Hamed's comprehensive definition of happiness. "To be pleased with one's own self " When and how was someone pleased with their own self? Anyone who hadn't even one star in a sky full of stars might be pleased with their own self. Hysterical laughter came to Abdolah again but he controlled himself and stared at his wife.

Manijeh was ready to answer Bahman's question. She was studying sociology at university and knew by heart many ideas from ancient and contemporary philosophers, from post-modernism to post-structuralism. When she had a chance she sometimes talked about them to friends or to Abdolah. She had a big mouth, and was proud of her ideas. Manijeh had read a lot of definitions about many processes of life, difficult or simple. She could give solutions for many problems, but she was bewildered. Why couldn't Abdolah, with his master's in accounting, successfully find a job, although it was said his qualifications were in high demand in Canada. But he hadn't been able to find a job in his field. He had gained experience delivering pizza, driving a taxi, as a courier, running a discount store, but these kinds of experience weren't worth a cent in Manijeh's view. He was a bread eater instead of a breadwinner. Manijeh, who worked and studied in university, who commented on the opinions of many classical and modern sociologists, couldn't make Abdolah learn the discipline necessary to succeed. Because she was disappointed in him, she didn't respect his opinions. Even though he always worked, he moved from one job to another. His income was of no consequence.

Hamed finished his comment, but neither Abdolah nor Manijeh had heard him. They were busy with their own definitions and personal problems. Bahman and Homa, who were listening, didn't understand much. Homa didn't trouble herself to listen closely. She agreed without listening. She had learned from him during their life together, and she would swear by him and his knowledge. Happiness was evident in her pleased look, in her sleepy talk, in her languishing behavior. To be Hamed's wife was the symbol of perfect happiness. She was the last person to offer her comment about happiness. She approved Hamed's statement.

While Hamed was talking, Manijeh arranged sentences in her mind. She wanted to explain, using many philosophers to make her ideas strong and effective. She said, "I believe happiness is obtained by hard work and discipline. In my opinion, happiness doesn't descend from the sky for anybody. One has to try hard and have discipline in work. For example, the solar system, the four seasons, the fall and spring, The plants and trees. There's no fault in nature." She reasoned so much that everyone ran out of patience.

Abdolah said, "If the bald man was a doctor, he would cure himself. Give an example from your own happiness."

But, as Manijeh started to describe parts of her happiness, Abdolah raised his hand to say, "Enough." It was his turn to give his idea, which was that, in his opinion, happiness didn't exist in reality, but it could exist in dream.

This time Hamed laughed loudly. Abdolah said angrily, "Why are you laughing?"

"For the same reason that you laughed at me," Hamed said.

To stop the argument between Hamed and Abdolah, Bahman asked Abdolah, "Have you any explanation of your idea?"

"For sure I have," Abdolah said. "I believe in Omar Khayam's philosophy." And he cleared his throat and read in a loud voice.

"Come friend, let us lose tomorrow's grief
And seize the moments of life:
Tomorrow, this ancient inn abandoned,
We shall be equal with those born seven thousand years ago!"

Without giving the others any chance to say anything he continued,

"How long shall I grieve for what I have or have not
Over whether to pass my life in pleasure?
Fill the wine bowl—it is not certain
That I shall breathe out again the breath I now draw."

Abdolah's recital was interrupted by clapping and praise, which meant it was enough.

"I wish we had read poetry instead of talking about happiness," Bahman said.

"You made the fire, you should extinguish it, too, " Manijeh said. "It's better to sing."

And she was more interested in singing Marzieh's song but Hamed said, "Let the two others give their own ideas as a conclusion, then . . ."

Manijeh was annoyed. "Then it will be time to go to bed," she said, "happy people are supposed to sleep on time."

Hamed was insulted by Manijeh's remark, but preferred to say nothing. The woman and her husband had some stinging words for him, he thought. Perhaps his wife was right, people were jealous of him. Anyhow they had come camping to enjoy themselves.

"Homa gives her idea," Bahman said, "I'd like to be last."

"I don't have an idea," Homa said. "My idea is the same as Hamed's"

Everybody protested. Hamed said, "Homa should give her own idea, too."

Homa said, "In my opinion happiness is what you explained."

"What about yourself, " Manijeh said, "what is your own definition of happiness?"

Homa pondered for a while and said nothing.

Bahman said, "We're waiting."

"I'm happy," Homa said, "that's it."

Then it was Bahman's turn. Bahman began with the others' definitions and then he read, "Happiness is running after wishes, not to reach the wishes."

All of them protested.

Abdolah said, "Repeating sayings isn't a big deal. Give us your own idea."

"I don't have a clear idea yet, " Bahman said, "I'm studying and researching it. I'm asking people so I can find a comprehensive definition of happiness."

Manijeh couldn't stand it any longer. The song was flowing in her like a river. She let her voice echo in the silence of the lake. She sang a few songs from Marzieh, Elaheh and Homeira. They were all enthralled by her song and her loud, clear voice breaking the silence of the dark. They meditated on the song, a balm after the stinging words of before. When the fire died, the moon disappeared behind the forest trees, and the lake fell asleep in darkness, Manijeh stopped singing.

The group went back to their own tents. All of them were awake late in the night, thinking about happiness. Hamed was doubtful about what he had said. For the first time he felt he was not happy with his wife. To him, she seemed stupid and her stupidity was clear to everybody. He thought about twelve years of life with her, the many times that she had behaved like an illiterate person, blank to every aspect of life. Like a dog who knew what to do to please him. He envied Abdolah living with Manijeh, a woman full of knowledge, a spiritual intellectual. A woman with independent ideas and opinions. A woman complete by herself.

Homa lay down in her sleeping bag, listening to the silence, and found she didn't like her husband as she had done yesterday or during the past twelve years. The man was too proud of himself. He didn't consider anyone else, especially her. Only himself. She reviewed her past with Hamed, and remembered how many times she was ignored by him and regarded as no more than a housekeeper, how he never asked her ideas about a single thing. When she fell asleep a trace of a tear wet her face.

Abdolah regretted his own hysterical laughter. He shouldn't have hurt Hamed. He believed Hamed was a good-hearted man and deserved to be a happy man, even though his wife was so simple she sometimes appeared stupid. But his own wife was a woman with authority and a bossy manner. He glanced at Manijeh, who seemed to be sleeping, though in fact she was wondering as well. He saw a woman with admirable capabilities. Her voice, in the night's silence, had thrilled him. Her idea of happiness was thoughtful too. She seemed exceptional, and he wondered why he couldn't get along with her, even though she was always helpful and full of ideas about life, many aspects of life that he didn't care about. He felt happy in some ways and was sorry that he had always blamed her and denied her.

Manijeh pondered over her own remarks. She realized she hadn't said all the truth. She reviewed her judgment about her husband. The man wasn't so easygoing and worthless. During the almost nine years she had lived with him, he had done his best. If life in exile didn't work for him, it wasn't always his fault. She accepted that circumstances could affect a person's life, and for Abdolah they were usually against him. He had done his best, but . . . Manijeh promised herself she would be more supportive of her husband, less critical.

Bahman added a few definitions to his former notes about happiness. Alone in his tent, he opened his notebook and in the glow of a flashlight he wrote the definitions. His plan was to create an encyclopedia using the knowledge of people around him. In his opinion, ordinary people might have more interesting ideas than the knowledge collected in books. He was enthusiastically spending time and patience on this job. He could see a hundred or two hundreds years into the future, when his encyclopedia would exist in libraries and be passed from hand to hand. When sleep made his eyes heavy, he turned the flashlight off, put the notebook under his pillow, reviewed again the discussion in his head and felt something stinging his flesh. What did happiness really mean? Did he have the right to pose such a question? Who was he, who gave him authority, to question his friends? Not only might his question and his encyclopedia of knowledge be something ridiculous, his existence seemed like a joke. As sleep took him away, he thought, "Happiness is an illusion, I will tell them tomorrow."

NOTE

With material from the *Ruba'iyat of Omar Khayam*, Penguin edition, translated by Peter Avery and John Heath Stubbs.

Her Twin

Life is a beautiful custom

SOHRAB SEPEHRI

Six years, five months and three days after being hired, she was handed a lay-off form letter. It was a spring day. The trees, after a cold winter, were green again, and the city had put on a new face.

Roxi was riding in a bus along an empty street near her favorite park. A hope was sprouting in her heart. "I wish I didn't have to go to work. I would get off here, and stay the morning, even the afternoon, among these trees." In this open space, where trees surrounded the park like a wall, the grass was green, the sky a blue deep and even. Moments later the bus had passed the park. Scattered buildings, trees and passing vehicles were once more in her sight. Roxi forgot all about her unattainable desire. She thought about her long day ahead. The open book lay forgotten in her lap. She already felt tired. The nightmarish prospect of unemployment was like a dark cloud in the sky of her mind. She couldn't make it go away.

She had been working in the factory for more than six years. She knew the entire place like her own home. She had developed an affection for it, a feeling which once in a while transformed into hatred. At least she was happy she had a job; some income. She was able to spend her own money and this gave her some pride and satisfaction. She knew her job so well she could have done it with her eyes

70

closed. If only the nightmare of machinery left her alone, she might have worked with her eyes closed. But the nightmare kept her on her toes. She couldn't let anything go wrong. Her supervisor and the general manager were happy with her. She hadn't had a raise in two years, but their reasons were probably valid; economic crisis, etc, etc . . . And she didn't complain. In fact nobody complained. That was it. No place for any change. The giant automatic machine that was supposed to replace them was silencing them.

She heard about the giant automaton the first day she started working. When she came in for her interview, Mr Spencer, whom everybody called Frank (Roxi did the same following the others) told her the factory had ordered a huge machine that labeled the bottles. "Your employment is temporary," he had added. "No one can say when the machine will come. There is no way of telling."

Roxi had started her work with fear and anxiety. The supervisor was a middle-aged man from South Asia, and had lived in the country for years, would remind her on every occasion that she should be careful and not make any mistakes. His accent was thick and it was hard for Roxi, who was newcomer at the time, to understand him. He would send out a trail of words, and Roxi would look at him silent and intimidated. She would imagine he was talking about the automatic machine.

The woman who worked beside her was from Romania. She was middle aged, white, and not talkative. She would put the bottles that Roxi had labeled into a box. She always worked with her back to Roxi and she never dared to look or talk to her. During lunch, Ludmila would sit with her husband who looked younger than her. They would talk a language that Roxi didn't understand.

The first few days and months passed fast, Roxi absorbed in her work, careful not to make mistakes. She was in a world of her own. Bottles came to her hands like little mechanical men, and they would escape like little genies, sometimes slipping through her fingers. But most times she grabbed and labeled them. Gradually she became faster and better. She could finally tame those little magic bottles. She could start to let her thoughts wander and only work with her hands. She was able to leave the factory behind, go home, walk around, visit her past and sometimes she would go so far away that when she returned she would ask in surprise, "Reyhaneh are you still here?"

"Reyhaneh?"

"Have you forgotten your own name? Aren't you Reyhaneh?"

Roxi would sigh and say nothing.

It was during the first weeks that she had to . . . she had to—But then again for George, that Taiwanese supervisor who could not pronounce "Reyhaneh," she had to change her name. She talked about it to Nader.

Nader said, "It cannot be. Are you saying that we have to change our names? They call me Naider, it is their problem, not mine, I am Nader."

Reyhaneh smiled mischievously and said, "Last night when you were talking to Sam, you called yourself, Naider."

"I had to."

"I have to, too. I have to change my name for George. So my name will be easier to pronounce for him."

Then she realized without anybody telling her that George was probably not his real name either. She had heard many names from those countries and none of them resembled "George" or anything like it.

That night they stayed up late and thought about different names. Nader would not accept her point, he made fun of her. When he saw that she didn't pay attention to his arguments, he gave up.

"It's none of my business," he declared, "it's your name. Do whatever you want with it."

Reyhaneh reasoned that if she didn't do it, they might fire her. There was no reason why they couldn't. They could get somebody with an easier name, a name they could pronounce. Later on in bed she stayed awake thinking up different names. She wanted to find one that she liked. She thought of many names, names she had heard in this country, or had read in books—Lisa, Sue, Ann. She laughed at the last one. No, she wouldn't choose that one. She liked names like Nancy, Margaret, Arlene, and Anna. That reminded her of the book *Anna Karenina*.

She thought of herself as Anna. Anna . . . it had a nice ring to it. But it wouldn't suit her. All names were foreign to her. It was past two o'clock in the morning, but she couldn't find a name that she liked. She thought about her parents: why they had chosen her name? It was a beautiful name. Since she was a little girl, each time she introduced herself, everybody said it was very charming. She was sure that her name was beautiful. But from the first day she had problems with it in this country. Somewhere between being asleep and awake she remembered Roxana, one of her classmates in the last year of high school. She was from Soviet Azerbaijan. She had green eyes and golden brown hair. Roxana played the piano. She even performed at the party at the end of the year. Those songs had lit a fire in her heart. had become friends with her. She went to her home several times and listened to her melodies on the piano. Roxana died the following year from blood cancer. Years had passed since then. And Roxana was still nesting in Reyhaneh's memory with her pleasant music and the beautiful melody of her name. She had decided to name her daughter, if she ever had one, after Roxana. Her Roxana was never born. She had her name. In the morning, when she woke up, the first thing she said to Nader was, "I found the name I was looking for, Roxana."

Nader, who was ready to leave the house, said, "You know best."

She woke her son up to go to school. He was in grade eight. He had to stay awake at night and study for hours, so he could catch up on his English. Nader was helping him with his studies. She too would sometimes look up the meanings of words for him in the dictionary, hoping that this way she might add to her own vocabulary, but when days later if you asked her the meaning of some word she could not remember it.

She didn't say a word to Peiman about her decision to change her name. She had convinced herself that in order to keep her job she had no choice but to do so. There was some kind of shame creeping inside her and she didn't want to talk about it.

"Only in the factory," she said to herself.

And now after six years five months and three days, although she was called Roxi only in the factory, Reyhaneh had been transformed into Roxi. As if she had been dissolved from one body into another. At home when Peiman and Nader called her Reyhaneh, the name seemed strange to her. Years ago that name was the most beautiful and suitable name she could think of. Now it was abandoned. Eight hours of her day, she was called Roxi, and the rest of the day . . .

Nader opened a pizzeria, and Peiman went to a college in another city, and nobody was at home to call her Reyhaneh and now . . .

She put on her uniform and was walking towards her workstation. She felt that the factory was breathing in painful silence. The workers looked at her seriously with no smiles on their faces. They all stared at each other in unspoken fear. George gave her a letter. Roxi read the letter and immediately understood that she was laid off and the factory was closed. She looked at the worker beside her, who was a young man from Bangladesh and had changed his name from Zulfaghaar to Zul. He looked at her questioning eyes with a sad smile, as if to say, We are doomed, we are all doomed.

"What about the automatic machine?" Roxi asked. If she had heard that the automaton had finally arrived she would probably not have been as shocked; that the factory was to be shut was unthinkable.

It was like the news of the death of a loved one. The manager of the factory, a gigantic Canadian man, entered the area. Everybody called him Mr Smith. Mr Smith gathered the factory workers in an open space in the factory and gave them a lecture. She understood only the first sentence. She couldn't listen to the rest of his words. The death of the factory was like a heavy burden of sadness on her heart. She wondered why nobody cried. On the contrary, everybody was silent and indifferent. When Mr Smith said something (was it something funny?) the sound of laughter filled the space around her. Roxi was more surprised. "Maybe this is their custom," she thought to herself. "Even in death they laugh and make fun." She remembered the sitcoms on TV; laughter was heard every once in awhile for no good reason. She wondered why she was thinking of such things. When she saw everybody walking in the same direction, she didn't know what to do. Ludmila took hold of her arm and pulled her.

"Where?" she asked.

"Farewell party."

"A party?" No, she couldn't go to any party.

She wanted to sit in a corner and cry. Then she realized that she didn't have to stand behind that machine and label bottles any more. A breath that had stayed captured inside her for six years and five months was released. She remembered her beautiful park. That morning she had passed it, and it had left a magnificent and richly splendid memory.

She took off her uniform, put her lay-off letter in her pocket and got out of the factory. She waited for the bus, which was less frequent at this time of the day. The blue sky was like an umbrella above her head. A cold feeling was inside her, right under her heart. From the moment she knew that her bond with the factory was broken, she had felt it there. Many times she squeezed it. A morbid thought passed her mind; what if she had a heart attack. She took many deep breaths. She noticed the bus coming from afar. She smiled at the thought of going to the park. The coldness beneath her heart didn't lessen. The bus reached the stop and a few people got off and on. sat down and the bus started. Roxi's thoughts were far away. She stared outside. She saw a woman in front of her, right behind the driver. She couldn't remember where the woman had got on. She couldn't trust her own eyes. She blinked many times. Maybe what she was seeing was only in her imagination. But it wasn't. It was a woman exactly the same as she was; the same height and the same figure, it was as if she was seeing her own image in a mirror. She wanted to get up and touch her, but she didn't dare. The bus reached the park. The woman descended, and Roxi too involuntarily got off the bus. The woman sat on a bench under the trees; Roxi followed her and sat beside her. Several times she opened her mouth to talk to her, but the words wouldn't come.

The woman was as silent as a tomb, and she was looking off in space. A book was in her hands, the one that Roxi was reading, a young writer.

In the silence of that spring morning, the park, the trees and the open spaces between the trees were all deep in thought. It was an unusually windless day for this windy city. Roxi felt sleepy. She had the desire to lie down for a much needed sleep. Six years, five months and three days she had woken up every morning like a mechanical toy at the same hour. In the twilight hours of the morning, she had prepared breakfast for Peiman, made his sandwich, even sometimes cooked the dinner. Nader would still be in bed all this time. For the past three out of four years, she hadn't seen much of Nader either. When she did, he was still sleeping. Once in a while at parties, in their friends' homes or in their own home when their friends were over, or once a year at nowruz for a few hours they were together. The pizza business used up all of Nader and all that he had left for home was sleep.

Since she had seen her "twin" (she had given her this name) she was not able to think anymore. Thoughts were becoming lighter and lighter in a mass of condensed clouds in her head. All she wanted to do was to lie down under the trees and sleep. Although she had her own home; an apartment on the twenty-fifth floor of a thirty-six-floor building, beside a major highway where traffic was incessant like a roaring river. Roxi had no desire to return home. Her home was empty now, every moment of the day and night. Thinking this made her sad again, as if she were thinking of someone who had died, and this made her heart cold again. At this point as the desire to sleep became stronger she got up. She saw that her twin was walking a little ahead of her, she lay down under a tree and put the book and the purse under her head. Then she went to sleep. Roxi thought, I've messed up.

She didn't feel like sleeping anymore. She only wanted to know how long the woman would sleep there. She wanted to wait for her to wake up. At that moment she remembered that her real name was , a name that had so faded from her life that she had almost forgotten it. She could not even remember when she had last heard that name. In fact for a long time nobody had called her Reyhaneh. She even believed that she had become Roxi. Yes, she wanted to talk to the woman. She hadn't talked to anybody for a long time. And now she waited. Little by little she felt the colour of happiness in her heart, happiness of release. The happiness of being drowned in the green that surrounded her, the sky that was as blue as a child's memory and the birds whose songs did not bother the silence of the trees. At the same time, she was uncomfortable with this happiness. One should not be happy at the death of a loved one. Roxi was happy and was waiting for her twin to wake up. She sat there. She didn't know how long. She saw that spring changed to summer and summer changed to fall. The leaves on the trees became orange, yellow and red. They fell from the trees and Roxi's twin was still asleep under the tree. Maybe she had gone to her eternal sleep. Roxi came to herself only to realize that the woman had been covered with dried leaves.

Then she got up and went home. Her home was silent, not unlike any other day when she got home from the factory at six o'clock. Nader was busy in his pizzeria, cooking and delivering his pizzas. Their son, in another city, was wrestling with studies. She cooked for herself, she watched TV. She had to laugh at sitcoms that were not even funny, watch commercials for the thousandth time and cursed them. Then she took a nap and read the Iranian newspapers, called a few friends and had the same conversation. And then it was time to sleep; close to dawn, she would feel Nader's presence, sometimes his body smelling of sex. She would get up, go to Peiman's room, which was empty now, and sleep in his bed. She could still smell that smell in her sleep. She wanted to throw up, she would have a nightmare. She would dream of George who made love to Ludmila, she would dream Ludmila's husband had come to their place, looking for an Iranian girl. She would wake up. Remembering Iran, she would think hard but couldn't remember the name of the street where her cousin Nastaran was living. She would go back to sleep and would dream about the automaton that was set in their living room. She was scared of it. Nader was working with it. He wanted to make pizzas with it. She would get up with the alarm clock and leave for the factory without having breakfast.

She took a deep breath. It was wonderful that she didn't have to go back to work the next day. Then the sadness of losing a loved one captured her soul again. She didn't cry. She called Nader and gave him the news of the factory being shut down.

"What about the automatic machine," he asked, "didn't they order it?"

"I don't know."

"So you were only torturing me and yourself by imagining it?"

"That wasn't my fault."

She hung up. Her life was strangely empty now. The one who died had left Roxi with empty days and nights. She lay down on the sofa, remembering her twin.

She was lucky, she was very brave, she thought. She stayed under the trees till the leaves covered her and I . . .

She tried not to think about the future. The future was like the automatic machine. It was there and it wasn't there. It was supposed to come. It was coming and not coming.

Eleven years, seven months and eight days passed. Then Roxi became Reyhaneh again and she forgot the name Roxi. She passed away in a hospital in this city. Her husband, her son, and her daughter-in-law, who after six years of marriage still didn't want to get pregnant, were with her. They couldn't have known what was happening inside her. Occasionally they saw a smile on her face. Sometimes she would reach out a hand for something. Reyhaneh was still in her beautiful park. The same park that she had passed for six years, five months and three days. And every day she had wished that she would spend an hour among its trees and listen to the song of the birds. Reyhaneh was lying down now under the trees on the green grass, was waiting for the trees to change colour, and pour down their leaves in a gentle breeze. Reyhaneh saw her twin, she smiled at her and said hello. She was greeted back.

"Father, Reyhaneh is saying hello," Peiman said.

"To whom? To me?" Nader asked.

The twin said, "Not to you, to me."

Roya and the Water

She had seen the sea in her dreams, in movies and on television, but when she saw the real thing, she almost screamed. She had come a long way, passing through barren and rocky land, crossing countries uphill to drown herself in the sea and get rid of a useless life, a heavy burden on her shoulders, hard to bear. Suddenly the sea was in front of her. She couldn't believe that she was witnessing the real thing. Am I not dreaming? she asked herself, bewildered.

All her knowledge of the matter was based on what she had heard or read in books. She had wondered if a real sea would scare her away; could she get close to it, once she saw it? Was there a mysterious centre of gravity, which would grab her and drag her inside its depth, place her somewhere deep in its cold and silent waters. The stories and tales she had read had formed her idea of what she was now seeing.

She sat on a rock, helpless and wondering what to do; contemplating the small and big waves playing on the sandy beach. She was surprised that the sea didn't frighten her. The temptation to hit the waves wasn't fearful. She wished to sit there on the rocks for hours, perhaps forever and watch those gay and playful waves. She wished to sit there and dream and forget about her real life, monotonous chores without any joy or creativity.

Am I not dreaming? she still wondered. Is this the same thing I saw on TV and in films? She could hear the sounds of the waves, playful and joyful on the sand, telling an everlasting story to her. She remembered a poem from Molavi; saying the sea was turbulent because it was in love. She wished she could remember the whole poem, so she could recite it. Later on she forgot about the poem and listened to the rhythm of the waves, there was water as far as her eyes could see. Silence, and the sun in the middle of the sky; the caressing blue sky, without a scratch of a cloud.

Nature seemed untouched and virgin to her. The sandy white beach, like a soft bed, accepted the games of its waves. The waves touched the sand for a brief moment, and ran away joyfully. The dense water revealed secrets to her, as she sat watching the waves come and die. She remained in a state of unawareness, which was new to her. She wished to be in that state forever, for time to stop and her unity with the eternity, with the water, to continue forever. The decision to throw herself in the water still was with her, but without fear or excitement. Can I? The waves were calling to her mockingly, laughing, inviting her to their arms.

Later on, standing on the beach, she looked far away, into the horizon, for a ship or boat. When she found none, she was certain that the sea hadn't been conquered by human beings

The next moment, a boat appeared from afar. It seemed as if something extraordinary was about to happen. She wasn't even sure what she saw was real. Am I dreaming? she asked herself.

The boat with its tall sails sailed towards her. Loud music and chatter ceased when it reached the shore. The men and women in the boat waved at her. She stepped into the sea with an intense desire to get inside the boat and go away. "We're sailing far away," said a woman loudly from the boat. She cried, "Me too, I'd like to go faraway, I always wanted to go faraway, so far that nobody could reach me." When she reached the boat, the water had reached her chest, touched her body like strong hands caressing her. Why hadn't she gone into the sea earlier? Her body was in a state of languor and ecstasy. Some hands caught her and pulled her into the boat. She sat quietly, fascinated by the boundless sea. Eager to get acquainted with those in the boat, she looked at them. A pleasant warmth was still in her body, the sun shining on her and her light dress drying quickly. She closed her eyes and abandoned herself to the smooth movement of the boat. Men, women and children around her were talking and laughing. They left her to herself. With her eyes closed, she felt the light touching her eyelids. The water, like a soft bed invited her to an unknown eternity making her part of its lightness and everlasting movement. The temptation to throw herself in the water was still in her. She didn't know how deep it was. She opened her eyes and looked at the sea. The water was deep green. The movement of the boat wrinkled the calm surface. She imagined its surface with nothing moving on it, smooth like a mirror. Where did those playful waves come from?

Here, the water was so motionless and silent that it seemed like a hard metal. The water was asleep.

The boat moved ahead. She didn't even ask where they were going. She was enjoying herself with her eyes closed and her destination unknown. No longer an oil-press horse turning around a circle, repeating her daily chore. She was far from her family, her husband, her children. They belonged to another era and she had traveled to another world; a mysterious world, with secrets and hideouts. She thought if she went back to the shore she would awake from this pleasant dream, again face an ugly life that enveloped her. She made sure that this wasn't a dream and everything was happening in the real light of the day. Her long wished-for dream had come true. She was looking at the sea, sailing on it. Whenever she wanted, she could throw herself into its arms and get rid of the death in her day-to-day life.

Throwing herself in the water was becoming an irresistible temptation, like committing a sin. She opened her eyes, overwhelmed with fear and joy. The dark waves, like a green velvet bed. "Can I?" she asked herself. She let go of the fear and abandoned herself in the unknown joy.

The boat took her away. She must have fallen asleep, because when she opened her eyes, darkness was everywhere. There was no sign of any men or women on the boat, all of them had gone like in a dream. Alone in the boat, floating inside the darkness. The sea wasn't calm any more. High and low waves pushed the boat in all directions, the sails were torn, there wasn't a star in the sky. The sea lamp blinked faraway. She looked for something in the boat to steer it. She thought about oars, but because of the dark, she didn't know where she was. Tired, she sat in a corner. Helpless, she realized that she had reached the end of her life. Soon she would become a prey to the sea. Fear took her in its claw like a monster. The life which was a heavy burden to her a few hours ago, when she sought death as a refuge, now seemed beautiful to her. She wanted to scream. Perhaps somebody could hear her. She even tried it, unsuccessfully. Someone was pressing her throat, it seemed. Her voice was no match for the waves. Tired, she yielded. Once in a while, a faint hope arose in her that all this was just a dream, that she would open her eyes and be in bed beside her husband, her children asleep in their room. The day would start again, bringing with itself her chores, the travails and joys.

The reality was, she was inside that boat. Darkness had enveloped her, the waves were dancing on her fear. Any thought of this being a dream was killed by the dreadful movement of the boat. She had been captured by death, accepting, little by little, the abandonment of life. Sad and depressed, she sat there thinking. Her life was useless to her without joy. Wishes had never come true. She was yielding to death. She stared at the darkness. She regretted that she had never lived the way she would have liked. Instead of fighting for life, she had just dreamed and wished for death. She always went the way other people had told her to. Now she was in the claws of death and she realized that life could be most fascinating if she tried to live it. Everything seemed beautiful and grand to her, even the trivial. She hadn't been able to live like a normal human being. Her life was non-ending envy. She had lived in her dreams, far from life. Now she believed that this darkness and the sea were not a dream but reality. If she was going to die, that was not an illusion, but a fact. She wanted to give herself some hope that it was not true, that she was not going to die. Someone screamed inside her, the voice told her that death was round the corner, in the depth of the cold, dark water, waiting for her. That dream could be as strong and as cruel as life itself. She felt the bitter reality with all her being, with her skin, with her flesh. Her dreams surrounded her like life itself. The dream about seeing the sea, which she carried around inside her for years and years. She had imagined herself sitting in a boat not unlike this one, sailing on the green waters to an unknown destination. Now her dream had come true, but she was sailing to her death.

The boat turned over with an abrupt movement, she fell into the sea. For a few moments she tried to keep herself on the surface. She remembered how she had seen swimming pools where she took her children, had listened to all those swimming instructors who taught her children to swim. Many of those instructors had told her that she could learn to swim, but she thought what was the use? She never had time to swim. Now she practised all those skills she had once heard about. She tried to float on the surface. She tried to move her arms. She wanted to stay afloat. A heavy wave hit her and threw her a few feet. When she came to herself, she was in the deep of the water. She should have yelled. She was sure that it was all over. She knew that the struggle was useless. If I knew about the secrets of the sea, she thought, maybe there would be a chance for rescue, but now I have to go. I lost my chance to live as I deserved. The water squeezed her lungs. She abandoned struggling and let go, as she had always done in her life. As death took her inside its wavy entrails, she breathed a gulp of water. Still talking with herself, she blamed herself for this unpredictable death, like always, blamed herself one more time. No one was to blame she thought. She should have known better. The sea was like life, with its strict laws, she should have learned about them. She had always been obedient, and now the waves were stronger than her, and made her obey one more time. She, who never had any power, obedient and submissive, was sinking.

*

After examining the body, the doctor was sure that death had happened as a result of drowning in water. When he announced the cause of death, the family of the deceased looked at him as if he was crazy. The woman had died in her bed. Her husband was certain that Roya[1] had gone to bed before him. He remembered that she had been upset the previous night, because of some dispute between them—nonsense—a useless dispute, as usual, it wasn't worth talking about. He said that his wife was in bed beside him the whole night. And in the morning he found her dead. She hadn't even made a noise that would wake him up.

The doctor signed the papers, stating death had occurred by heart attack. But leaving the room, he turned and looked at the body one more time under a white sheet. "Believe it or not, this woman has been drowned in water."

NOTE

1. Roya is a female name and means "dream."

The Shadows

It was Gohar's burial service. Mr Mavadat stared at her as she was delivered into the ground. It was as if he was in a dream. Dreams had kept him busy all his long life. He daydreamed all the time. Gohar wasn't Gohar any more. She was wrapped in a white shroud from head to toe. She looked like a bundle, about to be left in a big hole in the ground. Mr Mavadat's four daughters and his grown and young grandchildren were crying and beating themselves. His near and distant relatives, his acquaintances and neighbours surrounded the grave. Mr Mavadat looked at them with a question in his eyes: "What happened?"

Gohar was laid deep inside the ground. The cries and screams of his daughters grew louder with each spade of soil flung on her. Mr Mavadat saw Sohrab in front of him, sobbing. He had covered his face with his hands and his shoulders were shaking. Mavadat was absentminded. A few minutes ago his eyes were wet with tears, and now they filled with astonishment.

That morning he had just arrived at work when Sohrab called. Haji Rasool answered the phone and then passed it to him, "It's for you, it's your son."

He listened to his son and jumped, as if an electric shock had come through the phone.

"When?"

Mavadat gave the phone back to Haji Rasool. "My wife passed away."

Haji Rasool stood up too. His big eyes widened, and he asked, "Was she sick?"

"Sick?"

Mavadat didn't know. Sometimes she complained about stomach aches, headaches, pains in her chest, pains in her legs. Sometimes she visited doctors and took medicines.

Mavadat looked for his coat, which was hanging behind him on the chair. He couldn't see it. Haji Rasool gave it to him and called Karim from the back of the store.

"Give Mr Mavadat a ride to his house. He won't find a taxi this time of the day."

Mavadat sat beside Karim in the Nissan minitruck. They drove through downtown streets. He was dreaming about his own past, watching his life piece by piece. He couldn't see Gohar clearly, she was lost somewhere. She was like a shadow, belonging to the past, a very distant past. He didn't notice that they had reached home. His daughter was crying loudly. The doctor was there too. He certified the death. Gohar was in the living room, lying by the samovar table, covered by a white sheet. Mavadat went to her, knelt beside her. His daughter stood aside and sobbed. She smothered her cries, wondering what her father was going to do. Mavadat couldn't believe Gohar was dead. That morning when he left the house, his wife was sitting by the samovar table, wasn't she?

Mavadat had to leave the house every day before six o'clock in the morning to get to the bazaar at eight o'clock. His house was in a suburb, far from downtown. He had built the house after he retired from his position in government administration. He liked living in a quiet neighbourhood, far from the city, where it was quiet and peaceful. But it didn't work. Sohrab finished high school and was accepted in the university. The tuition was high. His third daughter, Manijeh, separated from her husband and returned to their house with two little daughters, and occupied the second floor. His retirement pension wasn't enough as living expenses climbed higher and higher. It didn't even cover bread, vegetables and potatoes. Mavadat had to go back to work.

Mavadat knelt beside Gohar, lifted the sheet. He smiled at Gohar. He remembered that years ago, when they were young, Gohar's black hair had poured out on the pillow.

"Sleeping or awake?"

Mavadat stared at Gohar's face. He put his hand on her forehead. Her body was getting cold. His daughter, standing behind him, sobbed louder. A hand touched his shoulder. Mavadat looked at Sohrab absentmindedly and saw the tears in his eyes. Mavadat started to cry. He pulled the sheet aside, revealing the body. Gohar wore a dress in mixed colors, green, gray and yellow. Her black socks came up to under her knees. Her hands crossed her chest. She was peacefully asleep. Manijeh covered Gohar's body again and screamed. Sohrab held his father's arm, made him sit down on a chair. Mr Bahrami, retired like Mr Mavadat, was there, too. He didn't need to go back to work. He had a house in Tehran which he rented out. He was talking to Mr Mavadat, offering condolences, the words which are said on these occasions.

Mr Mavadat sat on a chair. He didn't understand what his neighbour was saying. He was thinking. He looked at the white sheet and knew that his wife was under it. There were noises in the house. The telephone rang, the doorbell rang. People were coming and going. Sohrab and Manijeh answered the phone. Manijeh's two little daughters wandered around their grandmother and among the others. Manijeh took them upstairs, but they appeared again. They were scrambling from the rooms to the yard and kitchen and asking questions that angered Manijeh. Mr Bahrami and Sohrab were talking. Sohrab led his father to the courtyard, which was empty under the hot sunshine of Mordad (July). Mr Mavadat stared at the gardens, which had no plants or flowers, just weeds. Since water became too expensive for Mr Mavadat to afford, he had abandoned planting the gardens and left them as they were. He had to leave the house early in the morning and returned late at night. What use were plants and flowers to him?

Mr Bahrami and Sohrab were talking about Gohar's burial. Sohrab had called for a hearse and they planned to bury the body before sunset. Mr Bahrami was saying that leaving the body unburied didn't make sense. Mr Mavadat could see his wife through the window. He imagined it all in a dream, one of the dreams which had filled his life.

Neighbours, acquaintances, relatives and friends who had been told of Gohar's death rang the bell. Manijeh's daughters opened the door. Mavadat was in the hallway. He answered to the words of condolence, sometimes asking himself, "Is it over? Is there any Gohar?" But he couldn't believe that more than thirty years of common life with Gohar were over.

He looked up to the second-floor stairs and saw Gohar, wearing a chador, coming down. Her chador was white, like the sheet covering her body. Gohar smiled at him without speaking. Mr Mavadat smiled too. He wanted to say, "What's the matter with you, playing games?" But he said nothing. He turned to the living room and saw Gohar's body. He still couldn't believe that it was Gohar's body under that sheet. Something lit his mind, he started to think about the previous night and that morning. He tried to remember Gohar, then he couldn't. He just thought about the very distant past; twenty years ago or more, when they were young and had just two children. Gohar got typhoid fever and lost her long hair. She had to wear a scarf at home to cover her baldness. Then her hair grew again, curly beautiful hair that she always kept short.

Mr Mavadat forced himself to remember his wife's hair, soft and wavy as it was when he married her, and curly as it was after typhoid fever. But he couldn't. Gohar stood by the door in the white chador, as if she didn't hear the cry of her eldest daughter, newly arrived with her three sons. Gohar stared at Mavadat. She uncovered her hair, lifting the chador with its end trailing on the floor, and said, "Look at me. You're not a stranger. My hair isn't wavy or curly any more. It's white. It's completely white. It's rough too, like a horsetail. I'm not young any more. I'm not the girl of thirty years ago. I'm more than fifty now."

Mr Mavadat smiled, wanting to say, "Why not fifty-five?" Yes, last month when he filled the application form for ration papers, he noticed that his wife was fifty-five and himself, sixty-two. He sighed and said, "I wish I had found a peaceful retirement."

Gohar was under the sheet again. The daughters cried and sobbed loudly. Mr Mavadat heard Gohar saying, "You're not the only person who works. You see that I'm working too. I have to wake up early in the morning, go shopping, line up for bread and milk for the children."

Every morning Mr Mavadat left the house before six o'clock. On his way he usually saw Gohar standing in a line. Mr Mavadat didn't know which lines or for what she was waiting to spend the money from his pension and his job at Haji Rasool store. Gohar used to say, "If I don't stand in these lines, I'll have to buy groceries from the black market, for which I'll need more money."

Mr Mavadat didn't complain. He had given up interfering in domestic affairs. He wanted a house far from the city in a quiet area to spend his retirement in peace, but that hadn't worked. Early every morning he and his wife had to leave the house. And every evening when he came back home, he was so tired that he just wanted have his meal and go to bed, to be able to wake up early again the next morning. He saw his wife rarely if he saw her at all. They lived together like shadows.

As they put Gohar under ground, Mr Mavadat asked himself, "Why did she die? What was her illness? When did she get sick?"

The doctor had said, "She was suffering for a long time."

"Why was she suffering?"

"Baba," Sohrab said, "didn't you know that maman had a heart attack?"

No, he didn't. Wasn't he dreaming? Was it true that his wife was dead? That bundle inside the ground, was that really his wife? He couldn't believe it. His daughters' and relatives' screams shocked Mr Mavadat. When Gohar's body was completely in the grave and the men started to cover her, Mr Mavadat became sure the body wasn't Gohar. If it was, it didn't look like Gohar whom he knew and had married, having four daughters and one son from her. He had to find out about this Gohar, she wasn't his Gohar at all. What was the relationship between this Gohar, buried under the soil, and his wife? Why did his four daughters cry so loud?

On the way back home, Mr Mavadat sat in Gohar's brother Abdolah Khan's car. Sohrab and his two sons-in-law sat in the back seat. They talked about different subjects. Mavadat was daydreaming. No, it's not true, he thought. It wasn't Gohar who died today. Then he asked himself, so, when did she die? I didn't hear about it.

Mavadat remembered his past, yesterday, the day before yesterday, last week, last month, last year, and he couldn't find Gohar in it. He didn't see any sign of her in his life. Sometimes he saw a woman covered in a chador, coloured or black, he didn't remember. He remembered her in different lines; the bread line, vegetable line, milk line, potato line, innumerable grocery lines. He saw her in a long line of women in coloured or black chadors. Sometimes there were a few men too. He saw Gohar in those lines, and she looked at him indifferently, like today, when he pulled aside the sheet from the body and she didn't look at him at all. Late at night when he came back home, Gohar was either upstairs, busy with her daughter and her grandchildren, or asleep. She covered her face with the sheet so as not to be disturbed by light. They slept in separate beds. He tried to remember when they started sleeping separately. He couldn't remember. Perhaps it was after the birth of their fourth daughter. But then Gohar wasn't thirty years old yet.

At an intersection endlessly lined with cars and heavy with smog, Gohar's brother Abdolah Khan looked at Mavadat still absentminded and quiet. He hadn't uttered a word since the beginning of the burial.

"I wish you patience," Abdolah Khan said. "I wish you and your children long life."

Mr Mavadat stopped daydreaming. He looked at Abdolah Khan, who was just two years younger than she, but looked healthy and young, far from death. Abdolah Khan continued, "As long as we have a loved one with us, we don't care about her, but when she's gone . . ."

Mr Mavadat couldn't hear the rest of what he said. A loud siren disturbed him. But that half sentence made him think, the loved one we missed! Which one? Did he mean Gohar?

Mr Mavadat was a hundred percent sure that the person buried today was not his wife. That person didn't live with him for more than thirty years under one roof. That woman might be Gohar, but he didn't know her. He didn't know why she died. Did she have cancer? Did she have kidney disease? Did she have a heart attack? What was wrong with her? Why did she die?

Mr Mavadat saw a shadow moving in the house. She woke early in the morning before he woke up. She turned the samovar on, to make tea, and left the house. Mr Mavadat rose and left the house very early in the morning. He saw Gohar waiting in the lines covered in a chador, coloured or black, he didn't notice. She was standing in a line, but what for? He didn't know. This shadow now was dead. But Mr Mavadat was sure that she wasn't his wife, the one who lived with him for more than thirty years. How many more than thirty years? He didn't know. He really didn't know.

The Last Scene

She pulled the curtain aside. The streetlights were off and darkness covered everywhere, except a high wall in front of her window. The wall was lit occasionally by cars passing. She listened to the sound of the street but heard nothing. She wanted to open the window and listen carefully. Inside, the apartment was quiet as well. Just the tea kettle on the stove hissing the whole day.

She dropped the curtain. Absentmindedly, she wandered into the apartment, a certain kind of longing in her eyes.

"Why are you so anxious?"

She didn't answer. She stared at him, as if she didn't see him, or as if she was seeing him for the first time. Alienation in his eyes. Not only in his eyes, but also on his face; in the wrinkles around his mouth and his eyes, in his black and thick eyebrows, in his deep eyes staring at her rudely and making her abashed; in his hands which had held a book in his lap; in his body getting more and more crumpled and now a weird shape, an unknown shape.

"You're anxious for nothing. He might have found somewhere else or another foolish person. Don't you know that there are many in this city who would be seduced by four flattering sentences and ready to sacrifice themselves? You're living in a dream. When do you want to open your eyes?"

She looked at him, but she didn't see him sitting in front of her, in a red sweater; and the collar of his shirt was outside the sweater. He gazed at her for a long time. His eyes pierced deeply into her, sweepingly from head to toe as if stripping her. Laying her down on a surgery table, a surgeon dissecting her, cutting her into pieces.

"You are still the same person. You haven't changed in ten years, twenty years. Time hasn't affected you. Your hair has turned gray. You've become old. But you're still as optimistic as you were at twenty. So, when do you want open your eyes and face the reality?"

She heard his words but didn't listen to him. She wanted to get up and sit by the window and listen to the sounds of the street, sounds of darkness, outside the window . She wished the street lights were on and she could see the shadows of people crossing the street. She wanted to be sure that he wouldn't miss her building and get lost.

"Do you think you can rescue human beings? What do you think? The era of heroism is over, is gone. Today, everybody should think just about his own self. Don't you see it's a flood, everywhere? Don't you see the whole world is drowning, and you're thinking about rescuing others?"

Abruptly his voice became louder, she jumped and stared at him, surprised.

"What's the matter with you? Why do you look dumbfounded? Are you anxious that he's late?"

"Shouldn't I be?"

"Why should you be?"

She didn't answer. She didn't know what to say. The alienation between them was like the darkness beyond the window. It didn't seem like they had lived under one roof for many years; their bodies and souls had interwoven into each other, as if borne from one single womb.

"Why should you be anxious? Did you have any responsibility towards him? Did you know him? Did you—"

Staring at her, he became quiet.

What did he want from her? What did he see in her that she didn't see in herself?

"Perhaps . . . "

"What? Why are you speaking ambiguously?"

"You didn't tell me how old he was."

"I told you. He was young. A very naive young man. He didn't know anywhere. He was a stranger to this city. He had heard your name. He was looking for you. And me."

"You gave him my address that I should rescue him from shiftlessness, from alienation? That I show him salvation. What do you think? That I'm a saint? A leader?"

"Aren't you?"

His loud laugh made her jumping again. She left her place and stood by the window again. She pulled the curtain aside. The darkness was heavier and the silence deeper, covering the street. It seemed there wasn't a street anymore, just darkness.

"Ha, ha! A saint! It's over. The era of redemption and miracles is over. The era of leadership is over."

She dropped the curtain and paced the room. His voice filled the room, her whole body and her whole soul. A strange voice, a voice inside the apartment, close to her ears, echoing off the walls and losing itself. It was lost in her, took her away; away to the past, to those sunny days that now seemed like bright spots lost in darkness. As if they never existed.

"You never want to change. Everything is changed but you're still living in your heroic dreams in a world empty of salvation, sacrifice and love."

And love . . . What a shallow and colourless word! When and where had she heard it? She sat down and looked at his face.

"Ha? Do you think that you are still living in the era of heroic actions? Why did you tell him my name? What can I do for him? What kind of miracle can I perform for him? Look at these hands. They can do nothing. They're useless. "

"Not even give hope? Not even a caress?"

"A false caress? Like a meaningless smile? Ha! Perhaps you expect me to give him hope with empty words for a vague future?"

"Why not? Sometimes there's a bright future beyond a vain hope. At least he would find a reason for living, even if it's in vain."

"Then, that's what you think?"

"Yes, I always think this way."

"So, because of that you're happy. A prosperous person; happy for nothing. Is that you?"

"Me? I don't know who am I. But I know that I can't bear a human being to be helpless and say nothing, do nothing."

"What should you do then?"

"I don't know."

"Send him to me? That I make him hopeful about a future that doesn't exist? That I make a crown of deceitful happiness and put it on his head?"

"Didn't you do that before?"

"Those days are over. Then it was possible to deceive people and send them to paradise."

"So, there was a paradise?"

"A deceitful paradise that was made up by dreaming people who needed victims; naive, helpless victims."

"Don't you think those victims were happier than the lost and wandering people? Like the one I met yesterday; on the verge of suicide; on the verge of falling. I wanted just to make him forget about suicide with a few cheerful sentences. I could make him hopeful."

"What then?"

"That he would continue to live."

"What kind of life?"

"I can't imagine what kind. It depends on the situation. It depends on what kind of people he would meet."

"For example people like you. A cheerful person like you?"

"Or like you. If you were there, you would have encouraged him to throw himself into the river."

"How do you know that?"

"From your words. You're not the same person I knew."

"Should I be?"

"Shouldn't you be?"

"I told you. You're still living in the past, in an era of values."

"Human values."

"All of them were words, empty words with nothing beyond them. Like an empty dark space. Throw them out of your head. The world has collapsed. Typhoons everywhere, earthquakes everywhere. Haven't you seen all of these? Haven't you felt them?"

She didn't answer him. She stood by the window and listened. His voice filled the room. His talk smelled strange. As if she was hearing it from a strange person, someone she had never known. Even the tone of his voice was strange.

"Are you still waiting? Perhaps . . . "

"Perhaps what? Don't be afraid. Tell me. Don't be ashamed."

"Perhaps in rescuing him, you're looking for something else in him."

"What? Tell me. You know me better than myself. You think that you know me better than I do. Tell me, don't be ashamed."

He didn't answer, and she could imagine what he was thinking about her. The thoughts were disgusting.

"I just wanted to help him, nothing else. And you—"

"Me? Excuse me. I didn't mean anything. I was mad. You shouldn't be so optimistic. You shouldn't give your address to a stranger. You don't know him, do you?"

"Yes I know him. I knew him yesterday, when he wanted to throw himself into the river."

"And you didn't let him to do that?"

"He was desperate and hopeless. He was young, inexperienced. He hadn't known the beautiful things of life. He hadn't had any share in life."

"The beautiful things of life? And you believe in them?"

Did she? No. Perhaps she did believe in them until yesterday, but not today, before him. She looked at him, he was weird. He was far from her. She had submitted her body and her soul to him for a long time. Now he looked hideous. No, she didn't believe in them.

"I did believe."

"And now . . . ?"

She didn't answer. She thought about the young man. He might be struggling in the river at this moment. Yes, just for a few minutes, and then . . .

The telephone ring made them jump. The man answered the phone. When he put the receiver down, there was silence in the room.

"Who was that?"

"Him."

"Where is he?"

He put his hands on her shoulders and wanted to embarrass her. She walked away.

"Where is he?"

"They took him out from the water. They found our telephone number in his pocket; the only address he had."

She sat down. A lump in her throat, no words, no tears, nothing inside her. He was still talking.

"He rescued himself. He rescued himself from a disastrous life. Today death is the only salvation."

She stared at a vacuum. Strangeness covered her. Darkness surrounded her heavily. She got up and went to the bedroom. She put on her coat and crossed the living room with a small sack.

"Where?"

She stood by the door, looking at him another time. He was a stranger to her.

Memorial

It was as if everybody in the room expected something to happen. People came in ones and twos, a man and woman together, a few women, a few men. They looked for a place and sat down. Two young men, one of them tall, and dark, the other one shorter, with a moustache covering his mouth, were serving the guests tea, coffee, date and halvah. The tall man served coffee and tea in styrofoam cups. The shorter one had a dish of dates in one hand and a dish of halvah in the other. They followed each other, stooped before the newcomer to offer their products. Tea and coffee were accepted more often than halvah and date. Some people held a date with two fingers and a cup of tea in another hand, apparently saying to themselves, what do we do with these now?

People looked around for someone to explain what had happened. They still couldn't believe what they'd heard. Meeting an acquaintance, they would shake their heads as a greeting and smile faintly. They knew one doesn't smile at these such ceremonies.

Chairs were set around the room, but not all were occupied. Some people spoke to their neighbours, others stared at nowhere in silence. They might not have known anybody in the room, had just come to pay a tribute to the deceased.

Apparently the deceased's family were sitting by the entrance door. But it wasn't clear what the relationship was among them or between them and the deceased. Nothing was clear. At least not for all of the guests. They were waiting to hear something. Someone should talk. In a normal ritual, a poem would be recited or at least someone would talk about the deceased's life. Nothing was clear yet.

A man with a large black moustache and a big nose, in a black suit and a gray tie, got up from his chair. Probably the representative of the community which had organized the memorial. It was two weeks after the death, the woman's suicide. Her burial ceremony had been done by her family. The man, who was not young, or old, mid forty perhaps, welcomed the audience. His welcome seemed odd. Nobody was supposed to be welcomed to these kinds of ceremonies. He corrected himself and said, "Ladies and Gentlemen, thank you all for attending Mrs Arfaie's memorial ceremony."

He continued, "I mean, the community thanks you."

He read a poem from Sepehri[1]:

"If there was no death
Our hands would look for something else."

So what? Did he mean that the death was a good thing? Was it to be accepted with pleasure?

Some people were listening to the speaker in the black suit, others were daydreaming.

Sorayya wasn't sure she had ever seen Mrs Arfaie, and she didn't believe she knew her. But when such a person committed suicide, she was curious enough to participate in the memorial ceremony. Perhaps she could see her photo and might recognize her. If she had seen her, she might remember her. In Sorayya's point of view, suicide wouldn't be an easy way to escape life. Especially if the person who committed suicide become regretful at the last moment and wouldn't be able to change his or her mind. Sorayya believed that life passed anyway and anybody could get along with it, as she herself did. There would be always a tomorrow after today, nobody knew what was going to happen. A miracle could happen and change things for good. Life was passing, time and age would bury everyone. Life was a process with a sure ending. It wasn't like a river, flowing forever, it wasn't days and nights following each other to eternity. Life was for a limited time, with an unclear ending that would come at any moment.

By the time Sorayya finished her thoughts, the middle-aged speaker had finished his speech. He had talked about Mrs Arfaie's character, which was unique and excellent. The words echoed in Sorayya's head like a school bell. What did he really say? Sorayya was bewildered by her own question. What did she expect him to say? He admired Mrs Arfaie as a devoted woman, a caring mother, and a loyal wife. Sorayya wanted to picture her in her mind. Was Mrs Arfaie really a devoted wife? If so, why did she commit suicide? Who would play the role of a devoted wife to Mr Arfaie? His new wife, probably!

Sorayya laughed at her own thought. Not loudly, but to herself. These kinds of ceremonies weren't the proper place for laughter and mocking. She should behave decently. When she heard that a woman in her forties, with a son, a beautiful daughter and a loyal husband, a perfect family, had committed suicide, a strange curiosity prodded her. A curiosity with a bitter sorrow. Sorayya was a logical woman. She viewed life very rationally. She believed that suicide was the most useless and the most distressful way to end life. The news about Mrs Arfaie's suicide made her thoughtful. If Mrs Arfaie had been a twenty-year-old woman, Sorayya wouldn't have been surprised. Young people were inexperienced and wouldn't know how to deal with life's difficulties, sometimes their suicide was predictable. But a woman at that age, more than forty, who had experienced different aspects of life, was not supposed to commit suicide. Why really did Mrs Arfaie commit suicide? She might had have a strong reason, but it was not clear to Sorayya.

Some woman, Mrs Farhat, started to talk about Mrs Arfaie. Obviously this woman wasn't supposed to commit suicide, Sorayya thought. She was talking about Mrs Arfaie's courage. Courage?

Sorayya was bewildered. What kind of courage?

"You know, ladies and gentlemen," she said. "Forough was a brave woman."

Sorayya was more bewildered. What was the relationship between Forough Farrokhzad and Mrs Arfaie? She looked at the person beside her, astounded! Ah, Mrs Arfaie's first name too was Forough. What a coincidence! But there wasn't any similarity between those two persons, although the speaker was saying that there was between Forough Arfaie and Forough Farrokhzad.[2] Both were brave.

Sorayya wanted to interrupt Mrs Farhat's speech. But she couldn't create arguments. Why was she saying those two people were alike?

"It's not easy, " Mrs Farhat said. "Just imagine yourself in Mrs Arfaie's place. I mean in Forough's place."

Sorayya was surprised again. She couldn't figure out if the woman was talking about Forough Arfaie or Forough Farokhzad. How she mixed it up today! She would have liked to be in Forough Farokhzad's place and write those eternal poems, but she couldn't. She did her best but it didn't work. The poems, even the words, weren't friendly with her. Words couldn't explain her feelings.

Mrs Farhat's speech again confused Sorayya.

"Did you find out about their relationship?" Mrs Farhat said.

Sorayya thought, what kind of a speaker is she? Why did she question the audience? How would they know?

"Both of them were poets, both of them were brave, both of them were in love with life, in love with humanity."

Mrs Farhat's words touched Sorayya. How pleasant when someone dies, commits suicide, is killed in an car accident. Then, in a ceremony at the memorial, many people, friends, relatives, acquaintances get together and say lots of good things about her or him. If I die, she thought.

She abandoned the thought. She didn't want to die yet. She had two sons and a husband to care for. She had to work, make money. She had to work at home too and run the family. How would her two little sons grow up without a mother? She didn't want to die or commit suicide. Mrs Arfaie's suicide was hard to believe. Sorayya felt it was hard to breathe easily, as if she couldn't send air to her lungs.

Someone was sobbing. She looked around and saw a young girl, almost a teenager; with a skinny face, wavy hair, and black-rimmed glasses. She wondered, is she Mrs Arfaie's daughter? Mrs Arfaie might be like her daughter in old age. "And my mother who was like me at my old age."[3] She smiled at her own thoughts. She was supposed to be sad at a memorial ceremony. She should show some sympathy towards the deceased's family, but she didn't. She was more anxious and astounded than sad.

"I knew this woman for years," Mrs Farhat said. "I knew her in Iran, then here. She always was the same person. She didn't change. I mean the new society didn't change her. She was Iranian and remained Iranian."

She died an Iranian too, Sorayya thought. The most important thing was that she died an Iranian. She lived for a few years outside of her homeland and didn't blend into this society. She died an Iranian. I'll die one day too, Sorayya thought. As an Iranian for sure. But she preferred to die in her homeland. She didn't like to be called Iranian or not-Iranian. If she died in Iran, she would be a fellow citizen, an Iranian without any need for someone to emphasize her citizenship. On her gravestone would be written: "Sorayya Saatchi: Birth such-and-such, Death such-and-such," nothing else. It wouldn't need to mention that she was Iranian, she died Iranian.

Mrs Farhat didn't want to end her speech. She spoke about Mrs Arfaie's good moral character. Then there was a pause.

"I wish I hadn't seen her, " she said with a lump in her throat. "I wish I'd never known her. Her memory won't leave me for the rest of my life. I wish I had gone to see her more often these last days. I wish I had known she had such a decision in her mind. But I didn't. Swear to God, I didn't."

Sorayya was surprised. Why did Mrs Farhat emphasize so much? Why did she swear to God? As if she was seeing Mrs Arfaie's spirit in front of her, not believing her. Sorayya looked at Mrs Farhat carefully. She was sure that she was talking to Mrs Arfaie's spirit.

It wasn't imagined. The spirit was there. Sorayya saw her too. Why did she think she hadn't seen Mrs Arfaie? She had seen her in so many places. She had seen her among the small Iranian population in this city. Wherever there was a gathering, or a ceremony; most of them came. She had seen Mrs Arfaie, tall, slender, with wavy hair tight in the back, a skinny face, black eyes, narrow lips and small teeth. She looked worn out and old for her age, with gray hair, that made her look older. Yes, Sorayya knew her, had spoken to her a few times. In a poetry reading they sat by each other and exchanged a few words. It didn't seem like she had the idea of committing suicide. How is it possible to find out if someone who is sitting beside you and talks about daily life has such a terrible idea in her mind? Sorayya's mind was full of disturbing thoughts, but she couldn't talk about them.

Mrs Farhat is right to swear to God. How she's crying. She probably sees Mrs Arfaie's ghost. Yes, I see her too. Look, she is flying in the room. She's looking at everybody. She's standing in front of the man who spoke about her at the beginning of the ceremony and talked a lot about her nice character. How she's looking at him. It seems he sees the spirit and is confused. He's murmuring something. What kind of memorial is this? It looks like a ceremony to summon the spirits. I think it's Mrs Farhat's fault. She wasn't supposed to swear to God. No one forced her to do that. Why is she crying. Everybody is crying. Me? No, I'm not crying. I'm scared. My hands are cold. My face might be pale. My heart is throbbing. If I faint here! What would the others think about me! Wouldn't they think that I was faking? Yes. They would think so. Mrs Arfaie wasn't my relative, my dear aunt or my close friend. I saw her once or twice. We've only exchanged a few words, very ordinary words. Words which fill people's lives.

Her poor daughter is going to kill herself. There's nobody to take her out of the room. Perhaps she sees her mother's spirit too. What torture her husband bears! He might blame himself for the rest of his life. Shouldn't he? There's something wrong with him too. God knows how much he abused her to wear out her patience and force her to drink the glass of poison.

Oh, my God. Mrs Arfaie's spirit is looking at me. Perhaps I said something wrong. There's nobody to tell me; it's not my business. I've no idea about their relationship. Praise God. Mrs Farhat's speech is finished. She's wiping her tears. Mrs Arfaie's spirit has sat down in a corner too. It's not clear what she is waiting for. Why doesn't she want to go back to her grave and lie down there? She's dead now, she has to leave the living alone.

She is coming towards me. She sits in front of me. I'm scared to death but I have to be calm. Perhaps she has something to say me. Why me? It might be because I didn't believe these people; not that man's speech nor Mrs Farhat's. What can I do? It's not my fault. They were lying for sure.

Mrs Arfaie's husband is talking but I can't hear him because Mrs Arfaie's spirit is sitting in front of me.

"Don't believe them. Don't believe one word of what they say."

I say, "I don't. If I did, I wouldn't have summoned you from your grave to come here."

I become quiet. I don't know if I am right to talk about my real feelings. I feel sorry for her. She is a sad spirit. Her daughter's loud cry and the gloomy face of her son and her husband haven't any effect on her. It seems she has withdrawn from this world.

She says, "Why didn't you finish what you had to say? Are you afraid too?"

"I'm afraid. Were you afraid too?"

She laughs loudly. I'm surprised that she's laughing. I'm embarrassed. My heart beats faster. I barely keep from fainting. The noises change to a wheezing in my head. It seems the ceremony is over. The spirit leaves the room. I want to follow her, stop her and ask her: "Did you laugh at me, or . . . "

She looks back at me. She is sad and gloomy. "All of you are funny. Absolutely funny. I'm laughing at your funniness."

I laugh too. Not loudly. I'm afraid to laugh loudly and hurt the feelings of the mourning people. I laugh inside myself. I hear my loud laugh. I don't hear a voice except my loud laughter.

The memorial ceremony is over. Everybody is gone. I too leave the room. The wind slaps my face.

NOTES

1. An Iranian poet.
2. Forough Farrokhzad, an Iranian poet.
3. A poem by Farrokhzad.

Trial

He heard the doorbell and got out of bed. He put his jacket round his shoulders and went down the stairs. The Khordad (June) morning was spread across the yard and the trees whispered in the breeze, giving news of the coming day. Sparrows made joyful music with their chirping.

On his way to the gate, Goodarz thought he might be mistaken. Who would knock on the door this time of day? A passenger? A pedestrian? But he continued towards the gate, which was at the corner of the yard, hidden under the shade of an acacia tree.

He hadn't reached the gate yet, when he heard the bell again, echoing through the yard in that early morning. No, I'm not mistaken, he thought. His wife, too, had come out, she was at the balcony. Goodarz opened the gate, nobody was there. The dawn's opaque light lit the street. Gates of houses were closed. Goodarz looked around. A man appeared from where the street curved and stood at a corner. The man saw Goodarz and gestured at him to walk beside him. Goodarz hesitated. He put his jacket on, over his pyjamas. Was it bad to go out into the street in this outfit? he thought. Even though nobody was around, he was still hesitant. The man gestured again. Goodarz walked out into street involuntarily. He left the gate half open and went towards the man.

"I didn't believe you would dare come out of your house," the man said.

"Why?" Goodarz asked.

"Don't you know?" the man said.

Goodarz was astounded. "Something happened?" he asked.

"Follow me," the man said.

Goodarz looked at his pyjamas, wanting to say, "I'd better go change my clothes." But he said nothing and followed the man.

They reached an intersection that wasn't familiar to Goodarz. It wasn't more than a few minutes since he had left his house, but he didn't know the area. Where were they? he thought. He had lived all his life in this city. Why didn't he know this intersection close to his house? The man stopped for a while at the intersection. No cars, no pedestrians in view. All shops and stores were closed.

Goodarz wanted to ask, "Where are you taking me?" but he didn't.

The man turned into a street on the right. After almost three hundred steps, they entered an alley, with shops on both sides that were closed, but their wares were on display, accessories, scarves, socks, underwear.

I haven't seen this area, Goodarz thought, it looks like a bazaar, but it's not the city's main bazaar.

They went into the alley, into the darkness, night reemerging. They reached a completely dark place. Goodarz couldn't see the man, just heard the sound of his steps advancing in the darkness. I'd better go back, Goodarz thought. But how? He didn't have any idea how he had reached here. He only remembered how he had opened the door to the man, it was morning and his wife was on the balcony, listening to the bell, surprised.

Suddenly the man stopped by a door and pushed a button. A moment later the door opened and they entered a yard with windows around it—all lit. The man stood in the middle of the yard, by a pond of dark green water smelling of slime. Goodarz saw a few goldfish swimming in the water. They swam on the surface of the water and opened their mouths as if begging for air. Goodarz watched the goldfish and noticed a few of them were dead, out of the pond.

"Choose one of these doors," the man said formally. He pointed to the windows and continued, "Choose one of these rooms. You will be tried in the court."

"Tried? For what reason?"

"You'll find out."

"But I didn't do anything wrong."

"You'll see."

Goodarz was bewildered. Which one should he choose? All the rooms had the same window and an opaque light. When the man noticed Goodarz wondering, he ordered him firmly, "What are you waiting for? You should choose one of the rooms. I give you a free choice. And you don't have the right to complain. If you take a year, you choose for yourself."

"What's the difference?"

"I don't know," the man said.

"I don't understand, "Goodarz said, "why did you bring me here? Where is here, anyway? I've lived a long time in this city, I was born here. I never wanted to leave this city. I know it like my palm. But I haven't seen this place."

"It has existed since you were born," the man said, "if you haven't seen it, that is your fault."

"Perhaps I don't know the city well," Goodarz said, "perhaps I need to know it better. Now, that I'm retired, I have more time to do it."

"That's not a bad idea," the man said, "but now that you're here, you'll know here. Now you should choose one of these rooms and enter. The men in the court are waiting for you."

Goodarz wondered again why, on the first day of his retirement, they had called him to a court in this unfamiliar neighbourhood. As he pondered more, he didn't remember any wrong; thirty years of civil service without break, one-month vacations that he rarely used. A couple of times sick leave, one for an appendix operation and another when he was diagnosed with typhoid. He was an obedient, dutiful, punctual employee. What more did they want from him?

"Don't think too much," the man said, "it's better to choose one door and enter to clarify your situation."

"I don't understand," Goodarz said, "I can't understand at all. All of this is a conspiracy."

"Don't philosophize. All people pass this trial. Why don't you know about it?"

Goodarz asked hesitantly, "So, you are the secret police?"

" We aren't secret police. All people of this city know us." He said coldly, "You're wasting your time. In fact, you don't have a right to talk here. If you have any defense, you can make it in one of the rooms which you choose."

Goodarz looked around. Nothing was clear inside the rooms, there was just an obscure light in the windows. Goodarz chose the third room from the right. The man smiled mockingly and said, "You're welcome."

Goodarz walked towards the room. A heavy wooden door separated it from the courtyard. He wanted to open the door but hesitated. The man wasn't there, no one was in the yard. He decided to go back. He looked around, all doors were alike. He encouraged himself and turned the knob. The door opened heavily. Inside the room, behind a big, black desk was a man sitting on a chair. Beside him were two women, one on either side, in black dresses, their hairs covered with black scarves. They looked like twins.

Goodarz sat on the only chair, not very close to the desk, without greeting. He put his hands on the armrests.

" So, you retired?" the man behind the desk said.

Goodarz said nothing. He felt suspicious and decided not to cooperate.

"You came to the court of your own will," the man said, "you knew that one day you would answer to us. You should make it clear to yourself. You aren't as innocent as you think. In fact you are no different than a shadow; a mobile shadow. Never wanted to look at who you are. You were always a shadow and now you've become a still shadow. You retired. You don't need to go to your office every morning and come back in the afternoon. Now you can stay home and will soon be a shadow dying in the dark. But before dying you should answer. You know very well that you have to answer."

"What answer?" Goodarz asked. "Have I killed someone? Did I commit robbery?"

"It's not necessary to kill someone, or steal another's money. You have to answer to yourself. You should make it clear to yourself. Now I will read my question clearly for you. This is the question that you should ask yourself. We waited a long time. We were patient with you, but you never had the guts to ask such a question of yourself. Now listen carefully. I'll read my question and then suggest a punishment. You have choice about your punishment. As we left you free to choose your court, you have choice of punishment as well."

The man paused and after a while asked, "Are you ready?"

" Yes," Goodarz said involuntarily.

The man said, "Have you been happy with your life during thirty years of work? Have you been satisfied with your way of life and the fruits of your life? Just in one word, say yes or no. You don't need to philosophize about it."

Goodarz wondered, who was pleased with his or her life? What a stupid question they were asking him! He wanted to repeat the sentence. The man said formally, "Just one word, yes or no."

"No."

"You make trouble for me," the man said, "you've learned to lie to yourself. If you were not pleased with your life, why didn't you do anything to make it better? Why did you do the same thing all your life. Why did you stay in the same place like a piece of wood rotting. For this lie you should be punished."

"What kind of trial is this," Goodarz said, "that you don't give me a chance of defend myself. You don't let me talk?"

He turned to the women sitting in either side of the man like statues and said, "You tell me something."

The woman at the left side said, "Has your wife had any effect on your life? Did she try to change your way of life?'

"My wife was busy with her own life," Goodarz said angrily. "She had no right to interfere with my life!"

The woman on the right said, "We too just make note of the boss's words. We have no right to make a decision or interfere in your destiny."

"I told you at the beginning," the man said coldly, "philosophizing can do nothing. You know that you are guilty and have to be punished. Now you choose."

"At least give me a chance to make it better," said Goodarz.

"How do you want to make it better?"

How? Goodarz pondered.

"You see," the man said, "you don't know how. You only know that you weren't pleased with your life. But you did nothing. You never tried to stretch your feet longer than your rug.[1] You didn't give yourself any move. Now, how do you want to make it better? Isn't it better to make it clear to yourself and define your punishment and go your way? We aren't idle here. Many people are waiting for their turns. Look."

One of the women got up and pulled aside the curtain behind the man. Goodarz could see a crowd of men and women in the yard.

Goodarz asked under constraint, "What kind of punishment should I choose?"

The man smiled, satisfied, and said, "To kill one of your organs. The one which you think you don't need very much; arms, legs, eyes, ears, the sense of touch, taste, or thought. You have a few minutes to think about it."

The woman on the right rang a bell, and a deep silence dominated the room.

Goodarz pondered. He thought about his five senses. All of them seemed necessary; even more necessary than usual. Now that he was getting old, he needed his senses more than before.

The sound of a bell echoed in the room's silence. Goodarz jumped in his chair.

The man said coldly, "Well."

Goodarz said hesitantly, "I give up my thought. I don't think I need it any more. Without thinking I would feel freer. At least I don't need to think about good and bad in my life and won't be tried in a court."

The man smiled suspiciously and said, "I knew it. Thinking is futile. It's better to kill it. Well, goodbye."

Goodarz got up and stood in front of the man for a while and then asked, "Don't you give me a paper to certify that I've been punished and nobody will come for me?"

"Don't worry," the man said, "our trial won't be registered anywhere. It is just once; once and forever. The convicted never commits his or her crime again."

Goodarz came back home. Everything was the same as when he left the house. He imagined his absence hadn't lasted more than a few seconds. His wife was still on the balcony. Noticing him, she returned to the room. Goodarz climbed the stairs. He was tired. Retirement was good, he thought. He could sleep as long as he wanted. He put his head on the pillow and fell into a deep sleep. His wife went to his bed at noon, to wake him up. But she found Goodarz dead.

Two Sisters

I was shocked. My hands and feet seemed frozen, as if I was paralyzed. But I was conscious of what was going on, I realized they had come to arrest Saeed's mother. Well, I considered myself Saeed's mother. I mean I was, wasn't I? I had raised him for eighteen years. I never doubted or denied my motherhood. But my sister . . . I don't know what happened to her that night. We had never argued about Saeed, since his birth, we didn't have to talk about it. But that night . . . Perhaps I should show them more evidence. Those three men didn't take my words seriously, they didn't believe me. Well, she was his biological mother, not I. I just raised him like my own son. He was my only child. Akhtar gave him to me, the day she gave birth to him. We both agreed on the matter. He was her fourth child. Akhtar didn't want him, she wanted to abort. And I couldn't bear a child. After six years of marriage, I had no child. My sister had two sons and one daughter. Akhtar used to say, that's enough for me. I can't take care of four children. She visited a midwife to abort. The midwife wouldn't do it. Too late, she said. I was with her. I wanted to tell her, don't abort it, give it to me. I wanted to take the child, but not for myself. I wanted to raise it and give him back to her. I was sure I would never bear a child. I'd visited several doctors and all of them were as sure. Mahmood, my husband, wasn't worried about it. He believed it was God's will. We can do nothing about it.

I spent most of my time at Akhtar's house. Her children were mine too. But one's own children are something else. In the evening when I would go back home, my house looked empty. Sometimes I was so upset I cried. Mahmood soothed me. Happily, he wasn't the kind of man who would look for another wife to have children. He loved me. My husband was a cousin of mine. My sister, too, had married a cousin.We married the same night. Two sisters for two brothers. First Masood asked for Akhtar. He was the elder brother and in love with Akhtar. My father said I should get married first because I was the older one. So my uncle asked for me for Mahmood, his younger son. I wanted to continue my studies and get my diploma. Akhtar wasn't interested in education and didn't have good grades. My father didn't urge us to marry soon. He used to say, get your high school diploma, get a job and then get married. But it didn't happen as my father wished, because Akhtar and Masood fell in love with each other. When my father was told, he had to accept their wish. Our marriage ceremony was on the same night. I wasn't in love with Mahmood. I liked him as a cousin, he was a nice man and never insulted me. After a few years of marriage we found out we couldn't have a child. He didn't mind too much. He said, "What's the matter with our lives without a child? Suppose you leave a bunch of children after you. What's the difference?"

Well, he was a man. Perhaps he couldn't feel it. For me it was different. Not having children really hurt me. When I saw my sister put her breast to her child's mouth, the baby as if sucking her soul and her life, their blood mixing, I could feel an unimaginable relationship forming between them.

After Akhtar gave the baby to me, I celebrated the seventh night of the baby's birth and called him Saeed to match Akhtar's other children's names. To tell the truth, Akhtar never mentioned this child. The child didn't know that I was not his biological mother. He considered Mahmood and me to be his real parents. Well, we were. The only difference was that I didn't give him birth. After he was born, he was mine. I didn't nurse him either, but many mothers don't nurse their children. Akhtar did. She nursed three of them, for a year, or a year and a half. She nursed Nahid just one year, and then was pregnant with Saeed. My Saeed. She had a bad appetite during her pregnancy. She hated food, couldn't bear anything in her stomach. That was another reason why she wanted to abort it. I don't know what happened to her, why she decided to give the child to me. I didn't bring it up. I couldn't believe she'd think about it. My mother always used to say, "The children are like fingers on a hand, no matter which one hurts, there's no difference, the pain is the same."

I couldn't imagine that she would give her baby to me, but she did. As I said, I was always at their house. She wasn't against me. I helped her take care of her children. She had seen the desire in my eyes.

I remember the day very well; we were in the kitchen. We had come back from the midwife's office. Akhtar was upset and chain-smoked. I smoked with her. My sorrow was something else. I said nothing. I should have advised her to forget about aborting, but I didn't. She noticed tears in my eyes, and she probably felt pity for me. Akhtar always felt pity for me. She soothed me. "What do children do for their parents? What do they give except trouble? Look at our parents. They raised five children. Who stayed with them? All got married and left."

I was aware of these things. I knew that when a child grows up, it will leave. But a family still had grace. When we went to visit our parents' house, Akhtar with her children, Ali, Ahmad and Hassan with their wives and their children, the house was crowded with children. At every Idd we used to get together. Mother was always busy, knitting for her grandchildren or taking care of them when one of her children wanted to go to a movie or a party. Sometimes I was asked to take care of the children, but not very often. You know what I mean. My sisters-in-law didn't like me very much because I was a sterile woman. They were afraid I might hurt their babies. I suffered because of their behavior. I loved my nieces, I wasn't going to hurt them. Akhtar wasn't like that, or Masood. Whenever they wanted to go somewhere, they asked me to stay with their children. I wished the others left their children with me. The kids liked me. My sisters-in-law didn't care for me also because of the intimacy between my sister and me. Even though I like my sisters-in-law, there is a big difference between these two kinds of love. A sister is something else. Especially Akhtar. We had a particular love for each other since childhood. I loved her very much. She was my parents' youngest child, two years younger than I was. I didn't feel any jealousy towards her, nor she towards me. Even after marriage we stayed the same. As I mentioned earlier, she married the older brother, and I the younger one. That didn't cause any problems. Our husbands were two nice men. We had no complaints about them. We praised God we had good lives. When Mahmood was alive, I didn't feel I needed anything. It was more or less the same after his death too. He left me his pension. I'm a teacher. After I married Mahmood I continued my education and got my high school diploma and became a teacher. With just two of us, Saeed and myself, there weren't many expenses. We didn't have our own house—Mahmood didn't feel that having a house was urgent. He was happy with what he had, he was not a greedy person. Like a dervish.[1] On the other hand Masood is a man of business and money. He has his own construction company. He builds houses and sells them and makes a good profit. He became bankrupt once, but he recovered. Masood built a three-story house for his family, the house where I live too.

When Mahmood had a stroke and died, he wasn't even forty-five. God's will or destiny, I don't know. I couldn't believe it. He wasn't sick. Just a little tired. He came home from work and had his dinner as usual. He had some pain in his chest. He lay down to rest and the pain got worse. We didn't even have a chance to take him to the hospital. It happened so quickly. He never had a serious illness. But, usually, he wasn't very joyful either. He was mostly lost in his reveries. A book would lie open in his lap, whether read or not I didn't know . . . He wasn't very intimate with the child either. I don't mean he didn't love him. He loved him very much. But not as I did. I was dying for him. I never told anybody that he wasn't my real child. The child didn't know either. When Mahmood died, he cried for him as if he was his real father.

Later, I had to tell him the truth. I told Akhtar that it would be better if the boy knew about his real father. Something disastrous was going to happen. Akhtar told me they had fallen in love before we went to live with them, when they were younger. Nahid is older than Saeed, who was the last child.

Saeed talked to me about his love. He was very close to me. Since his father died, I mean since Mahmood died, he had got even closer to me. He has a special love for me. I have always thanked Akhtar. Without Saeed, I wouldn't have known the feeling of having a child. Yes, I was very happy. When he told me he was in love with Nahid, I felt the ground slip under my feet. I talked to Akhtar. She was shocked too.

"What do we do then?" she said.

"It's better they know the reality," I said. Then we decided to tell them that they were brother and sister. Saeed didn't want to believe it, didn't want to accept it at all. Nahid was more mature and wiser. She realized their love was impossible. Hamid and Majid, too, talked to Saeed. The four of them were religious. Not believers in Hezbollah, but real believers. They prayed, read the Koran and discussed it. Maybe religion helped Saeed forget Nahid's love. Otherwise . . .

Well, praise God. Whatever it was, it didn't raise a scandal. Imagine, marriage of a sister and a brother. Who can accept it? I would have probably killed myself. What did my poor sister do to be caused this suffering? Anyway it was over for good. Religion or wisdom or caution, something helped them forget their love.

That nightmare had just finished when the government started to persecute and arrest political activists, especially the young ones. Akhtar became anxious. She knew Hamid and Majid were politically active. Nahid, too. It wasn't hard to find that out. She would put on a tight veil, leaving home early in the morning and coming back long after school was over. It was clear to us that she had some business other than high school. Masood had gone to Europe to find out about universities and living expenses and about sending Hamid and Majid abroad. Here, the colleges and universities were closed. I think the kids became involved in politics because they had nothing to do. Saeed was in grade eleven but he got involved too.a year had passed since we'd moved to my sister's house. My landlord needed his apartment back and we had to move. We looked for another place to rent, but couldn't find a suitable one, the rents being so high we couldn't afford anything. My sister's house is big, with rooms and a small kitchen and a bathroom on the third floor. There is a big balcony which I like very much, from which I can see a vast sky behind the window, and there are short walls separating ours from the neighbours' balconies.

My sister said we could move into her house and have the third floor and pay whatever we could. I accepted. Saeed was happy too. He spent most of his time with my sister's children. The problem with Nahid had started some time before, but living in my sister's house, I found out about it. Well, praise God that it finished with a happy ending. But the problems never really ended. Akhtar's agonies and Akhtar's children are mine too. And I love Nahid as my own child. I wouldn't want a stranger to come and take Saeed or Nahid away.

But you see . . . they came and took all of them away. Not only Nahid, all of them. We didn't think the problems with the children were serious. In fact, the children didn't say much. There had been some comings and goings which we couldn't explain. Sometimes they came home late and left the house very early. Sometimes they brought their friends and stayed up late into the night. When Akhtar questioned them, they gave confused answers and said, Mother don't worry. I tried to comfort Akhtar that to be religious wasn't an offense. But she said, I'm afraid they'll make trouble for themselves.

Majid was in the third year of engineering and Hamid in the first year of agriculture college. But well, what good was it when the universities were closed and students were wandering around? Nahid was still in high school. She would put her maghneeh[2] on tightly. I mean she had to, because if she didn't, they would dismiss her from school. She didn't care about her courses. What use were they?

Akhtar wanted to send three of them abroad. Then she looked at me and corrected herself, four. Nahid said they wouldn't go and their father was wasting his time over there.

Nahid was right—they couldn't leave the country. They came and took them away. Saeed and I were in our room. Saeed was busy with his homework. I was knitting—a habit picked up from my mother. Akhtar never knitted. She didn't work outside the house either. She didn't like knitting or sewing. For me, knitting is a relaxation. When I knit I meditate or daydream. That night, the sky was cloudy and I wanted it to rain. When Mahmood was alive, on rainy evenings, while the kettle was humming on the stove, it seemed as if the rain was singing in the drainpipe, and I knitted. Mahmood was always reading. Sometimes he read to Saeed. He read him Nima's and Eshghi's poetry.[3] I would say to him, why are you reading these hard things to the child, he won't understand them. He would answer, he might not understand the concept, but he will enjoy the rhythm and rhyme.

As I said, that night I was knitting. The weather was getting cold. I'd closed the window, and the sky behind the window was cloudy. I heard the first-floor bell. It was past eleven. I looked through the window and saw that the gate was open in the yard. Perhaps Akhtar or the kids had opened it by the remote button. I saw a few men rushing into the house. My heart sank. So they had finally come. I looked at Saeed who was busy with his homework. I told him to hurry up, to get dressed and flee to the neighbour's house. He didn't even have a chance to ask what happened..

I don't know how he ran away, but he did escape. I stood in the middle of the room in a state of shock. Then I regained myself and collected his stuff, pushing it under the bed. Yes there was just one bed in the room, which Saeed used while I slept on the floor. There wasn't room for two beds. I turned the light off and lay down on Saeed's bed as if I was asleep. I heard their voices coming up the stairs. They turned the light on and saw me. I rubbed my eyes, as if I had wakened up at that moment. They asked me if I was living alone.

I watched them astounded, my tongue a piece of wood in my mouth. One of them looked around the room and then . . . I don't know what happened next, someone seemed to call him from the first floor and he left. Then I lost consciousness, or I fell asleep. When I opened my eyes, I saw Akhtar standing beside me, weeping and beating herself, saying they had taken the three. What about Saeed, I asked her. I don't know, I didn't see him, she replied. Then I remembered that I had urged him to run. I went out into the balcony and looked around, but he had gone, I don't know where.

The following days and nights were a nightmare. Akhtar didn't know what to do, where to go to look for her children. Masood called to know about his family and she told him about the children. She also told him that Saeed had run away. Why did you talk about it over the phone, I said to her. Don't you know that they listen to the phones? But she was not aware of what she was doing.

That night they came again. The same scene. Two weeks later three people rushed into the house again. Were they the same three? I don't remember. Do I remember anything from the first night? No. I swear to God, it was as if I saw them in my nightmare. Saeed called and told us that he was in a secure place, but he didn't tell us where he was. We didn't ask him either. Both of us talked to him. We were happy that he had been able to save his life. But for how long?

They came again late one night and again there were three of them. Two came up, the third one was in the car. One of them asked, who is Saeed's mother?

I was shocked. What did they want Saeed's mother for? Neither Akhtar nor I were political. We were busy with our lives. The children, well, they weren't children anymore that we could control. One of them looked in our eyes and said, which one of you is Saeed's mother?

Again, it was as if my tongue had become a piece of wood in my mouth. Well, I was his mother. I'd raised him. She just gave birth to him. She had him nine months in her womb and then gave him to me. That was our word to each other. And I couldn't believe she would keep her promise. Whether it was going to be a boy or girl wasn't important for me. Well, she saw for herself. I was not sad anymore after Saeed and didn't envy other women's children, and actually gained weight. I knitted for the baby and bought some clothes.

Yes, the man looked into our eyes and asked again, who is Saeed's mother?

Well, what do you think I should say. I should say, I am the mother. But I wasn't. I wasn't his biological mother. Do you think that in that moment I realized why they asked for his mother? No. My tongue was locked. I was scared to death, and my whole body was trembling

The man asked for Saeed's mother for the third time and now he was yelling. What do you want his mother for?

The man said, are you his mother?

I said, yes I am. What do you want me for?

He said, get ready and don't talk any more.

Akhtar said, wait a minute. I am his mother. I mean I'm his biological mother. She just raised him. She looked at me as if she didn't know me, alienation in her eyes.

I said, Sister, what are you saying? Have you lost your sanity?

She didn't look at me. She said to the man who was pushing me to the door, Yes, I gave birth to him and then gave him to her to raise him, well . . .

The man looked at me and then at my sister and said, How do we believe you?

Akhtar said, why can't you believe me? Are you going to distribute halvah[4] to us that we should argue about it? As I said, I'm his real mother, she just raised him.

I couldn't believe that Akhtar would make me feel worthless in front of those enemies. I couldn't understand what was going on in her mind. Something in my throat wouldn't let me talk, and rendered me mute. I couldn't defend my motherhood, the eighteen years labouring after Saeed. Yes, I wasn't his mother. The truth was with Akhtar. I couldn't change the truth. Those two realized that Akhtar was right. I was shocked. My sister just had a moment to put her black chador on before they pushed her out of the house to a car parked by the gate. She didn't even turn back and say goodbye to me, as if she was afraid of looking at me.

Later on, when I regained myself, I thought about it a lot. Do you think she did this to me because she didn't want me to suffer for her child. I don't know. But I still consider Saeed to be my own child. He's my son, and I wish they had taken me instead of Akhtar.

NOTES

1. a dervish is a person who is not materialistic.
2. a maghneeh is a certain kind of veil covering the head and shoulders
3. Nima and Eshghi are two famous Iranian poets.
4. Halvah is distributed among the poor on religious days.

Unkind Hands

"Me? How would I know her? Among thirty or forty thousand Iranians in this city, how could I know her? No, I haven't met her, or heard her name."

Angelica said, "You have a fellow countrywoman upstairs in intensive care."

Should I be curious? I was very busy as usual. Angelica had finished her shift. She took her white uniform off and had black tight pants on with a loose sweater reaching to her knees. Her dyed hair was yellow and combed on top of her head. Her blue eyes were deep, and looked tired and red-veined. She spoke with her accent, "Go and see her. She can't speak English. She just said she was Iranian."

I told Mr Mehran, "You should do something for her. You, as director of this association . . . "

"Not an association, assembly."

"Assembly, association, organization, what's the difference? You have responsibility."

"My job is voluntary. I don't have authority here. I can do nothing."

"If you don't do anything," I said, "who then can I ask?"

He stared at me with cold, glassy eyes. He had clean new clothes on. A dark blue tie, with coloured patterns. His shirt was striped, gray and white. His coat was gray as well, with some white in it. His pants,

I don't know, I didn't notice. He was sitting on a rocking chair, relaxing. His thick lips were wet, as if he creamed them with Vaseline, or wet them with his tongue. His eyes were cold as glass.

"Was she your relative?" he asked.

Angelica said, "You've a fellow countrywoman."

"What are you talking about?" I asked her.

"In the intensive care department—a patient in critical condition. She doesn't speak. She doesn't know English."

I stood by her. Sleeping, she had her hand on her chest. She had an agate ring on her finger.

"She hasn't been conscious since she was brought to the hospital," said Dr Lee. "She just said a few words and fell unconscious. We don't know anything about her. They brought her from the street."

"From the street?"

Mrs Mehrparvar was the head of a feminist association. Big? No, obviously she was on a strict diet. She asked, "Coffee or tea?"

"No difference," I said, "I have an important thing to say."

"Ms, this kind of work isn't our job," she said. "Burial? What's the relationship between women's rights and a burial?"

She wet her lips. Her lipstick looked darker. Many wrinkles were under her eyes, but she had lots of undercoating. A cream powder the colour of bronze covered her face, her neck and the wrinkles around her lips. Her look seemed that of a stupid, quiet cow, yielding to everything.

"The dead have rights, too," I said.

Her void eyes, empty of thought, widened a little. A cold and meaningless smile appeared on her mouth and she asked, "What did you say?"

She hadn't understood. I realized she didn't understand. It's always the same, the foolish people get the top jobs, leaving no place for the smart ones. The smart ones always hidden away in corners. Somewhere remote. It might be their own fault. They show more sensitivity, more care, than is necessary.

There was nowhere to talk about the matter. Mrs Mehrparvar got up from her chair. I don't know if she noticed disappointment in my eyes or not. Perhaps I was like a cow, too. She wore a lawn-green shirt, a gray skirt, a white jacket, and a scarf in green, red, yellow and purple. Everything suited her. She was like all managers.

Standing by the door, I looked all around the room, everything was in order and matched Mrs Mehrparvar's dress. The chairs were dark gray, the frames were pink, a dark pink, but the space seemed empty. Empty as a vacuum. The potted plant beside the window was stretching to a dead light. On the walls were women in different costumes with different coloured frames and a dead smile carved in their faces.

I stood by the door and said goodbye to Mrs Mehrparvar. A feeling of alienation, like a glow of cold light, covered me. A feeling of alienation that was in the space. The woman with her big body, with her belly tightened as if screaming, "Release us, we want to be free."

I looked at Mrs Mehrparvar; her smile carved on her face, like the smile of the women in the frames. I asked myself stupidly, "Is she beautiful?"

She said, "If you don't have any relationship to her, why do you make trouble for yourself?

The woman was unconscious. Dr Lee said, "She had a stroke, or she has been shocked. Her heartbeat is not normal."

Angelica changed her shoes, wearing her boots; black boots, black tight pants inside the boots, a green and black loose sweater, mixed colours. Her heels sounded in the hallway.

"I have to get home early," she said, "my son is waiting for me. My son doesn't eat breakfast if I'm not home. He stays in bed."

She left her husband in Poland when she came here to see her sister, and didn't return.

"I found a job. In those days there was a big demand for nurses. I stayed. I wrote to my husband to come here, he didn't. I got a divorce.

I won't marry again. Getting divorced is harder than getting married."

"Go and see her," she told me. "She's just said one word—Iran."

"An identity card?" I asked. "Does she have anything to show who she is? Where is her home?"

"Nothing," said Dr Lee. Writing on a paper in his hands, he eyed me. He took the woman's hand, and said, "She's gone." He wrote some more, his eyes hidden under his eyelids.

The woman was tiny on the hospital bed, as if sleeping in a garden, under a shady tree. Had she gone to paradise? Death had such serenity! Why hadn't I seen her? In this city, with thirty or forty thousand Iranian immigrants and refugees, why hadn't I met her? With so many programs for Farsi, had she come and I hadn't seen her?

"Come in the evening, " Sorayya said. "Bahman, Hossien and Sedikh will be here too. Bahman is working in a big organization. Maybe he can do something."

"May, may, may. It's too late. She must go to Iran. She must be buried."

"Iran? Is it easy? That takes a lot of money."

"I knew her, " Farzaneh said. "She was Soheila's mother."

"Soheila? Which Soheila?"

"You don't know her. She's left. A few years ago she left."

"Why didn't she leave then with her daughter?"

"I don't know. I didn't have any connection with her. When Soheila was here, sometimes I saw her at Soheila's place. She came to clean the house. When Soheila left, I didn't see her any more."

"Where did she live?"

"I don't know."

Sue said, "We keep her just twenty-four hours, no more. That's the hospital rule."

"We're nobody," said Mr Mehran, "we don't have authority to take action, we don't have a budget. Burial costs money. Didn't you know that? Why don't you inform her children? How many children does she have?"

"Four."

"With four children, she is left lying on the ground?"

"In the hospital morgue."

Mr Mehran wet his lips. Touched his tie. His tie didn't need to be touched. He tapped the desk with two fingers, slowly, in an indescernible rhythm. His fingers were chubby and his wedding ring had sunk in. Black hairs sprouted on his fingers like weeds.

"If you don't do anything," I said, "I mean if you can't do anything, whom should I ask? Please tell me."

"Why are you involved in this matter?" he said. "You're saying she has four children. All of them are grown up."

"I don't know where her children are," I said, "I don't have any addresses for them. They aren't living in this city."

How did I know. There are thirty or forty thousand Iranians in this city.

"Tell me how many Iranian are in this city, " I asked him, "you should know that."

He laughed. Soundless mocking laughter. Was my question funny? What a stupid look he had!

"Do you have her home address?" Mr Mehran asked.

"How?" I said. "She wasn't my mother."

"It's strange, " he said, "with four children she is still lying on the ground."

"In the hospital morgue," I corrected him.

"When the soul leaves the body, it starts decomposing," said Dr Lee, "all cells start to decompose and die. The complex organization of the body falls apart abruptly. The nervous system loses outside and inside connections. Heart stops to work and cells begin to decompose."

"Does decomposing have any beginning?"

"Decomposing is the beginning of death, beginning of corruption and nonentity."

And the woman yielded to corruption.

"I knew her," Farzaneh said, "She was an intelligent and reserved woman."

"What do you mean by intelligent?"

"I mean she was a woman who read books, who had a point of view on every thing."

"She was traditional," Sorayya said, she used the English word, "traditional."

"There's nowhere for these words to be spoken here, " I said, "we have to do something for her, send her to Iran."

"Why Iran?" Bahman asked.

"She wanted to be buried there."

"How do you know that?" Sadekh asked, "you say you don't know her."

"Louise told me," I said.

Louise had a pink and gray striped shirt; the donut-shop uniform. Her complexion was neither black nor brown. But her hair was curly brown. Obviously she had dyed it. Her teeth were white and glowing. There was a certain sadness in her laughter. Her voice was husky, as if she had a cold. She said, "Pity for her, she was a nice woman." And her eyes were full of tears. "Was she your mother?" she asked.

"My mother? No, I don't have a mother."

"She told me she had one daughter and three sons."

"Where are they?"

"I don't know. She told me, but I've forgotten. Far away, very far. She said she wanted to be buried in her homeland."

"So why didn't she go there to die?"

"Death doesn't inform you. It wasn't time for her to die."

"Sixty or fifty-eight?"

Dr Lee said, "She had no papers to show how old exactly she was. She should be around fifty-eight or sixty."

"She looks younger," I said.

"Death makes you look younger and then decomposing will begin. Decomposing is the beginning of death."

"Don't you even know her house?" Bahman asked.

"How would I know?" I said. "I didn't know her."

I had to explain. I have to explain every detail.

"Where did you get to know her?" Sadikh asked.

"To know her? I didn't know her at all. When I saw her, she was dead, she had begun to decompose."

"Why do you talk confusion?" Sorayya said.

"You're killing me, " I said, "all of you. Whom do I ask for help?"

"It has nothing to do with you," Farzaneh said.

Angelica had a dark red sweater on; long and loose. Her pants were gray and tight; tucked into her boots. Her yellow hair was darkened. She had red lipstick on. Her blue eyes were deep in her cheeks. Smiling, she asked, "What have you done to your fellow countrywoman?"

I thought about the woman. She was frozen, like a stone. She had begun to decompose. She had become a stone.

"Have her children been informed?" she asked.

"It's too late," I said.

"Her daughter left this place," Farzaneh said, "I didn't see her anymore. Sometimes I met her at Soheila's house. She told fortunes from Hafez."

"Don't you have any address for her daughter?"

"At the beginning she wrote me a letter. Then she stopped."

"Why didn't she go with her children?"

"How should I know? She didn't want to go. Should she have gone? Did my parents follow me?"

"But she came here."

"She might have thought that was enough. She came to take care of Soheila's baby. When Soheila was pregnant she came and stayed. Then her two sons were here too. I suppose they left too."

"Suppose?"

"I think they left. They left before Soheila."

"And you're not sure of anything?"

"Nobody is."

But I was sure that the woman was my fellow countrywoman.

"You have a fellow countrywoman in the upper floor." said Angelica.

She didn't have her purse with her; it might have been lost or stolen.

"Mrs Mehrparvar, won't you stand up for this woman's rights?" I asked.

Mrs Mehrparvar laughed. The wrinkles around her lips and her eyes were clear; and I stared at those wrinkles. Mrs Mehrparvar got it. She was an intelligent woman. She wasn't a cow. She smothered her laugh, as if she realized that laughing at such a topic was disrespectful. I asked her to help me with the woman's burial.

"Any person in this country has an identity," she said. "A social number which is like a birth certificate, a health number, perhaps some other numbers such as banks cards, credit cards. Why couldn't you find a number for this woman?"

"Do I have to?" I asked. "I'm trying to bury this woman."

"Here or in Iran?"

"Well, of course in Iran. Louise said, she wanted to return to Iran, but she couldn't. She had said, in Iran everything had become so expensive, life was hard, rents very high."

Louise said, "Let me sit. I have a break for fifteen minutes." She sat with a coffee in her hand.

Mr Mehran shook my hand. His hand was cold. His glassy eyes were wet. Had he cried? No, he had a smile on his face.

"Forgive me," he said. "The organization can do nothing."

Organization, association, company, when they do nothing, what use are they?

"Don't be disappointed," he said. "Her children will hear about it. Death has a loud voice."

"A loud voice?"

The woman was unconscious. Dr Lee said, "She's gone. Her heart is not working any more. Decomposing has started."

I looked at Mr Mehran. He saw the same question in my eyes again and said,

"Swear to God, I'm nobody. This organization and those titles are nothing. All of these are volunteer jobs. You know, there's no money in it. It's just decoration."

"What about the budget the government gives to this association?"

"This is not an association, it's an assembly. There's a big difference between an assembly and an association. An assembly doesn't have financial authority."

"So, why does it exist? Why do they waste your time?"

"What time? I feel proud to do something."

"So, why?"

"Don't ask so many questions," he said.

Angelica laughed. She had her soundless shoes on. She had on the white, nurses' uniform, which was loose for her body. She was skinny and tall. She always was on a diet, always worried about her body.

"They took her away," she said.

I wanted to ask, where? My tongue stuck in my mouth. I lost the words. I was only speaking in my mind, asking where?

Angelica understood, and said, "Iran. An insurance company came and took her away. It seemed she had a burial insurance and paid for it monthly. Tomorrow or the day after tomorrow they will send her to Iran. Over there someone might bury her."

The Wanderer

For Marzieh Asadi

The first time I saw the figure in a dream. I couldn't decide if it was a man or a woman. I can say it had no face. It had the features of a human being, it spoke, but its voice had a strange tone. The first time I saw it, it said, "I'm coming from past centuries."

I remember "past centuries" very well.

When I left my home, I saw it standing by a small alley. I was astounded, to tell the truth, I was scared. No one was in the street. I don't remember if it was afternoon or morning. The street was in a shadow and a chilly wind was blowing. When I saw it, I wanted to return home. But I thought it had nothing to do with me. It might have been waiting for someone. I passed it. I didn't want to look at it. But I turned and met its eyes and couldn't distinguish if it was a man or a woman, young or old. Even its attire didn't stay in my memory.

Its existence in that place was bizarre for me. I said to myself, "It could be an ordinary man, waiting for someone." I was scared and decided to go back home. I passed it, and when I was at a distance from it, I realized it was following me. I only sensed its being, its steps made no sound. Then I heard its voice. It asked me, without introducing itself, "Do you know where you are going?"

I was surprised. A stranger usually won't ask such a question. I imagined it to be someone bothersome. Now I was sure it was a man.

One of those troublemakers who get in a woman's way. I wanted to walk faster, but I couldn't. I felt I didn't have strength. Meanwhile I encouraged myself to face him.

"Walking fast is no use," he said, "you won't reach your destination."

And now I thought about my destination. Where was I really going? I stopped for a moment, as if oblivious of the stranger.

"You'd better stay here," he said, "I want to talk to you."

I turned back, looked at him and saw it clearly. It almost didn't exist. It only was a feeling.

"You always go," it said, "but you don't know where."

And I pondered. I didn't feel it any more nor hear its voice. I went back the way I'd come, hoping to find it by that small alley and ask it what it meant, but it wasn't there.

One may see something in reality and imagine it as a dream or illusion, or the opposite, see it in a dream and imagine it as reality.

*

Everywhere was light, like on a sunny day. I was among a crowd. I don't remember if there was a demonstration or a promenade or a picnic. I was in a vast place covered with lawn—not a rotten and crushed lawn but a very fresh and green lawn. There were some flowers planted in a few places and young saplings murmuring in the breeze. I don't remember why there was a huge crowd among young saplings and flowers . . . I saw a group gathered in a corner, singing or listening to a speech and clapping for a speaker, though only they had heard what he was saying. I was wandering among the crowd. I remember I was very tired and it was strange for me because I didn't look tired. I wanted to find a place to sit, but I couldn't find any. I had to sit on the lawn but I didn't know why sitting looked weird. Nobody sat. All were standing or walking. Even the people around the speaker moved, in a way, as if the speaker was pushing them to some unknown destination. Sometimes I joined a group. I mostly wanted to be a part of a choral group. It seemed thousands of songs were in me, and I never had a chance to sing them. But I didn't know why my voice couldn't adapt to the group's voice. I sang the notes in a wrong way, or I was left behind or was singing ahead. I couldn't be one with the group, even once. And because of that, I sang a few lines, and all of them looked at me strangely and I had to be quiet. At last I entered a big group in a vast area lit with sunshine and I started to sing with them. It seemed a beautiful song, as if I had heard it before. I had tried to sing it alone by myself, but I couldn't. This time I thought I was succeeding and I sang with the group. But I felt all of them become quiet suddenly and listening to me. I was encouraged and sang the song loudly. Suddenly I heard a voice. "You sing out of harmony."

I turned towards the voice and saw the same person. Again I couldn't distinguish if it was a man or a woman. Actually its gender wasn't important to me. But in that moment it was important to know the person. Sometimes the gender of a person affects their character. Everybody has a different prejudice about gender. I'm not exceptional. There's always prejudice of men towards women and of women towards men. Although I try not to judge people, it is important for me to know a person. It is someone appearing in my life and judging me.

When it said, "You sing out of harmony," the crowd looked at me, and then began to sing louder, out of harmony with my singing. And I tried hard to sing with them, but I couldn't. I had to leave the group. I was very tired. All day I had gone from one group to another one, no harmony with any of them and I wasn't interested in their games. Then I felt lonely. I wished to sit or even sleep, but sleeping or sitting among that crowd, which moved like a river, was impossible. Perhaps I was afraid to be crushed under their feet. I looked for an empty place, a place where I wouldn't hear a voice and could synchronize my inner songs, which struggled to come out. I had to make myself accept that to be in harmony with others wasn't an easy task.

I leaned against a young sapling and closed my eyes. I saw it again with the same unclear features. It was standing close to me and it said, "You're right. You can't be part of this crowd. You belong to another era. Your existence seems strange here. Why do you waste your time? If you want to find out who you are, you'd better follow me."

It was the first time it had spoken to me directly, looking at my eyes and with sympathy. I felt I wasn't tired any more. I was eager to follow it even though I didn't know where it might lead me. Still I wasn't sure about its gender, the way that it was dressed, its long hair, its slender and fragile body, its voice so delicate and caressing. It didn't scare me. But there was a vague feeling in me that it should be a man. Perhaps a prophet or a man from another world, or just an illusion. No matter what its gender was, it could make me follow it to an unknown destination. I, a person locked in place for life, had been able to disconnect myself from a strict and rigid routine that had surrounded me all my life.

I followed it for a long time. I didn't know for how long, but when I regained myself and looked around, I was in a place I hadn't seen before. A barren land with no houses, no trees, no sign of people. It sat and told me to sit too. I waited for a while and expected to continue after a short break. I closed my eyes just for a second, involuntarily, and when I opened them again I didn't see it any more. I just heard its voice, a woman's voice, it was my own voice, telling me, "Don't be afraid of solitude. Solitude is a vast world. Just be careful not to be lost in it."

The words touched me and made me calm. I just wonder why I hadn't heard it before. So I closed my eyes again and didn't want to open them any more. I had experienced solitude before. Solitude was really a vast world, but I didn't have the courage to step into it. In fact I was afraid of it, but I always thought, if one day I could kill my fear, I'd envelop myself in it and take refuge in it.

MEHRI YALFANI was born in Hamadan, Iran where she finished high school, before moving to Tehran to study at the Technical Faculty of Tehran. She graduated in Electrical Engineering and worked for the government and Tehran Cement as an engineer for twenty years. Mehri Yalfani began to write short stories in high school. Her first collection, *Happy Days,* was published in 1966, and a novel, *Before the Fall* in 1980. Mehri Yalfani emigrated from Iran in 1985, going to France and later to Canada. A collection of short stories, *Birthday Party* was published by Par Cultural Foundation in USA in 1991 and a novel, *Someone Is Coming,* came out from Baran Publisher in Sweden in 1994. Her first collection of short stories and poems in English, *Parastoo,* was published by Women's Press in Canada in 1995. *The Shadows,* a collection of short stories, was released by Afra Publication in Toronto in 1997, and in 1998 a novel, *Far from Home,* was published by Iranbooks in USA. Mehri Yalfani is currently working on a novel, titled "Moon and Soil."